Willow Trees Don't Weep

FADIA FAQIR

HERON
BOOKS

First published in Great Britain in 2014 by Heron Books
an imprint of
Quercus Editions Ltd
55 Baker Street
7th Floor, South Block
London W1U 8EW

A CIP catalogue record for this book is available
from the British Library

PBO ISBN 978 1 78206 950 8
EBOOK ISBN 978 1 78206 951 5

This book is a work of fiction. Names, characters,
businesses, organizations, places and events are
either the product of the author's imagination
or used fictitiously. Any resemblance to
actual persons, living or dead, events or
locales is entirely coincidental.

10 9 8 7 6 5 4 3

Printed and bound in Great Britain by Clays Ltd, St Ives plc

Typeset by Ellipsis Digital Limited, Glasgow

Willow Trees Don't Weep

The author of several novels including *Pillars of Salt* and *My Name is Salma*, Fadia Faqir was born in Amman, Jordan, and moved to Britain in 1984. In 1989, the University of East Anglia awarded her the first PhD in Critical and Creative Writing. She currently holds a writing fellowship at St Aidan's College, Durham University, where she teaches creative writing. She divides her time between Durham, London and Amman.

To my father, Ahmad al-Faqir, whose love of truth and justice, and struggle against oppression, have inspired my writing.

Part I   Behind the Poppy Fields   1

Part II   The Bombax Tree   71

Part III   Acid in the Milk   99

Part IV   Xanadu   125

Part V   Jerusalem in England   163

Part VI   Secret Whispers   227

Part I

Behind the Poppy Fields

The day was perfect for departures. It was dry as usual, the sky clear, sun shining, but there was a chill in the air that goose-pimpled you all over. *No Islamic funeral!* were my mother's last words, but my grandmother ignored her wishes. She asked our 'religious' neighbour, who was never allowed into our house when my mother was still alive, to wash her and perform religious rituals. I spent all morning spying on her, something that was second nature to me. She scooped water, reciting verses from the Qur'an, poured it over my mother's bald head, scrubbed her body with a loofah, performed her ablutions, dried her and then wrapped her scraggy corpse in white haj clothes. If she were alive and heard her say, 'In the Name of Allah, the Compassionate, the Merciful,' she would have gouged out her eyes.

My grandmother arranged for her coffin to be carried to the mosque, where they performed the Funeral Prayer, and then to be driven in a van to the local cemetery. Women were not allowed to go there, but she insisted. The driver sped over uneven roads and we huddled on mattresses in the back, holding on to the coffin.

'Slow down, you idiot!' said the imam. 'One more pothole

3

in the road and we will all levitate like astronauts in outer space!'

'This wretched van has no shock absorbers. A chickpea on the asphalt and you're flying.'

'The coffin will slide out if you're not careful!'

The cemetery was a flat, arid piece of land on top of a hill, dotted with slabs of concrete and white markers. The soil was cracked and there were no trees or plants, except for a few thorns that grew in the cracks or between the graves. Sparrows gathered when we arrived, craving a crumb or two. I walked behind the procession, holding my grandmother's hand. Tears ran down the furrows on her face all the way to her neck, soaking her knotted veil.

My mother's coffin was made of plywood – the cheapest my grandmother could find in the market – and the number of mourners was small. The local doctor, imam, grocer and his unhinged assistant, garbage collector and milkman lowered it into the ground. When it disappeared I gasped, breathed in, but could not cry. My insides were being carved out, as if by the special sharp pipe my grandmother used to empty the courgettes and aubergines before stuffing them with mincemeat and rice. She threw herself over the grave and began scraping up the soil. The local doctor blew his nose. No tears from me, Najwa, daughter of Raneen and Omar Rahman and granddaughter of Zainab! I stood there a cripple, unable to grieve for you, my so-called father, or for her.

4

Normally mourners gather for a meal after the funeral, but they all found excuses and vanished.

'I have to go to the dentist,' the unhinged assistant said.

'He's never been to the dentist in his whole miserable life.'

My grandmother and I were dropped by the mosque and we walked to our house under the warm midday sun. Children in the nearby kindergarten sang rhythmically, 'I am a bird, I could fly, I could also say goodbye.' I was not a bird and could neither fly nor say goodbye. Although I was free to breathe, walk, work, I felt like a prisoner, condemned to my life. The shoe repairer knew my grandmother well and threw a warm *salaam* at her. 'Long life to you!' She thanked him and asked him to kiss his youngest child, 'that crazy, kind rascal.' We bought some tomatoes for the salad, medicine for my grandmother's stiff joints and a hairband for me and went home.

When we arrived, my grandmother brewed some tea, added fresh sage and poured it in our best tea set, the one my late mother designated for classy guests and kept locked in the display cabinet. It was never used, for no one visited us. No male guardian, no honour, no status in this neighbourhood.

'Najwa, sweetheart!'

Sweetheart was an indication that the discussion would be serious. I tucked my fringe behind my ear, tied my hair and sat down on one of the cushions my mother had scattered in the garden. She used to arrange and rearrange them to make it look homely.

'Now your mother is dead, you have to go and look for your father.'

My father, Omar Rahman, who walked out on us when I was three, loomed large in the past, a featureless dark shadow, without eyes, lips or voice. I remembered very little: his strong, bushy hair, a scar at the end of his left eyebrow, the warmth of his bony fingers clasping my ribcage before flinging me up in the air. 'Why?'

'Because I don't have long to live and you'll end up alone in this house.'

'Don't say that, Grandma! And I have a job and can survive.'

'You know how it is in Amman and particularly in this neighbourhood. Chaste women don't live on their own. Tongues will wag. You'll be ostracised, *habibti*. And you have no relatives. As they say, "Better a man's shadow than that of a wall."'

'He's dead to me. They both are.'

'Don't say that!'

'He left us and never looked back. No cards or recorded messages, like the ones you hear on the *Greetings for You* radio programme.'

'It's for Palestinians, who cannot cross the Jordan River easily. My husband's family recorded one for me. By Allah, how I cried, listening to it.'

'Why would I go searching for him? He should look for me, his daughter.'

6

'Darling! He sent you letters, gifts and photographs, but my daughter – may Allah forgive her – destroyed or hid them.'

My mother used to spray the garden with water even in the winter and my feet would freeze as I swept the floor. A chill tingled through me. If she were alive I would have hurled myself at her. I ran to the bedroom, jumped into bed and pulled the quilt over my head. Her photograph, which my grandmother had blown up and framed, gazed down at me. Her cruel, kind, almond-shaped eyes seemed glazed, as if she were in a trance.

'Najwa! You're twenty-seven so stop acting like a child.'

You're as bad as each other. You abandoned me and she deceived me. My chest tightened, the muscle in my right cheek twitched and my eyes itched. I rubbed them, praying for wetness. They were dry.

When he left, twenty-four years ago, my mother changed. She took off her veil, cut her hair, packed my father's clothes, Qur'ans, books, prayer beads, aftershave, comb and tweezers in a suitcase, hurled it in the loft and forbade me from mentioning him. My grandmother told me that whenever someone knocked on the door I used to run, thinking it was my dad. 'The sound of your little feet tap-tapping on the floor fanned the embers in your mother's heart. She would unhook all the curtains and wash them by hand, hang them in the garden and watch them billow in the breeze for hours.

She cried over him for months, but she would wake up in the morning dry-eyed, put on her suit and trudge to school. She said that she had to hold on to her job to put food on the table. "Teaching the children, with their ready laughter, helps somehow," she said.' But that was when she started taking tranquillisers.

She would pop a pink pill into her mouth then fiddle with the towel until she calmed down. In the afternoon, after sweeping the concrete floor and washing it with water, she sat under the jasmine, sipping cardamom-flavoured tea and listening to Fairuz sing about a small café where young lovers regularly met. I shall remember her always arched on a plastic chair, her feet up on a stool, her head tilted back, eyes closed and hair cascading down, enveloped in a cloud of perfume and tranquillisers. It was a rendezvous with you, whoever and wherever you are.

One Friday, when I was about ten and spying on her, as instructed by my grandmother, I saw her climb a ladder to the loft, push the suitcase to the edge, pull it down and put it on the floor. She wiped the dust off with her hand, unzipped it and inspected your belongings. She held the prayer beads then pressed them over her heart, sniffed your shirts, perfume, comb, and flicked through your books. Then she closed it, put it back and took your books to the garden. She asked me to help her 'destroy this filth'. She cleared a space in an empty flower bed and looked over her shoulder. I handed her the books one by one: *The Islamic Caliphate*, *The Glorious*

Ottoman Empire, Overcoming the Fear of Death, Islamic Jihad, A for Allah, The Ideal Muslim Father and *Soldiers of God: With Islamic Warriors in Afghanistan and Pakistan*. She sprinkled some kerosene over the pile, struck a match and threw it. Instantly the books caught fire. The flames ate the pages, rose up and swayed, blackening the wall. She stood there watching until the heap turned into sheets of soot.

I knew I was different. I was not allowed to cover my head, wear a long school uniform or trousers, recite the Qur'an, participate in the Ramadan procession or wear prayer clothes and go to the mosque in the evening with the other children, who carried lanterns. I would stand by the iron gate, listening to them sing, 'Welcome Ramadan!' The house was 'secular' and it took me years to understand the meaning of that word. I stood out as if I had a birth defect with my unruly hair, western clothes and uncovered legs. Once, a schoolmate gave me a silver 'Allah' pendant for my birthday and my mother confiscated it and locked herself for hours in the guest reception room. 'No religious words, deeds, texts, symbols, jewellery or dress in this house!' my grandmother said and twisted her lips. Needless to say, I failed the Islamic faith subject every year. Don't ask me how I finished school and graduated! I just did.

My mother wanted me to study French at college, 'because it's the most secular country on earth', but it was not on offer so she spent days looking at the list of subjects taught at community colleges then decided that I would train as a tourist guide and work in one of the hotels by the Dead Sea, the most cosmopolitan and secular of environments. She was always on edge, her hands shook, chin quivered, eyes wandered. I could not tell her what I really thought, afraid that she might flip and trash the kitchen the way she did a few years ago. I saw myself as different from what she had planned or envisaged for me, but I was her only child, what was left for her, so I kept my mouth shut and went to college.

Our neighbour's son was always there. I went out in the early morning, walked to the end of the alley and waited for a public car or bus to appear. He was always there watching me from a decent distance. It happened every day until I began noticing him with his angular shape, shorn hair, large eyes and small ears. He wore the same white shirt and trousers, which shone with endless ironing. I would steal a glance at him and jump into the waiting car. It was my *salaam*. One day he did not show up and I got worried. Was he ill? Did he give up on me? Was I too stuck up for him?

Our 'religious' neighbour told my grandmother the whole story. His family married him off to the daughter of a Syrian merchant. 'Najwa is not marriage material,' his father said, 'because, rumour has it, her father is a drug baron somewhere on the borders of China. Also, brought up in a house without men, she wouldn't know how to show my son respect and tend him. Their's is a joyless house, with three shrivelling women rattling about in it.'

My heart fell, banged against the tiles and broke into pieces like a demitasse. I sat with my mother under the lemon tree. 'Why did he abandon us, leave us like this, fending for ourselves?'

'It's this ugly thing called religion. Allah is more important to him than us.' My mother gathered up her thinning hair.

My grandmother sucked her last tooth. 'Some say he got married to an Asian beauty and now lives like a king in the mountains of the Himalayas.'

My mother's chin quivered. She was still in love with you.

Soon after, she got ill and I had to give up college to find a job to make ends meet and help my grandmother take care of her. Her friend, the local doctor, arranged an interview for me at a hotel called Amman Tower through his connections. 'It should be civilised,' she said and ran to the toilet to throw up.

I rarely went to west Amman. I imagined a tower so high it blocked the sky, but it was just a small villa, clad with engraved white stones, with a beautiful garden full of palm and olive trees. The interview was brief. The owner, an old man with shrewd eyes, had one look at me and said, 'Hired.' He ran his finger along the worktop, checking for dust. 'You have to be punctual and ever smiling, like that battery. What's it called?' He laughed.

The Sri Lankan maid stopped polishing the brass. 'Ever Ready!'

'Yes.' I looked down at my mother's modest shoes, which she had allowed me to wear for the first time.

'Speak loudly and clearly!' He pointed his pen at me.

I hemmed. 'How much will you pay me?'

'That's clear enough. Four Jordanian dinars an hour.' He coughed then pressed his hand to his chest.

When I went back home my grandmother was waiting for me, wringing her hands. 'What took you so long?'

'One public taxi to the city centre, and another from there to here. The good thing is I didn't have to wait long.'

'How much would that cost?'

'Sixty piasters, more or less.'

'Without your mother's salary, we have to be careful.'

'By the way, Grandma, it isn't a tower at all.'

'Amman Tower is not a tower!'

'No, just a small villa with a lovely garden.'

She sucked her last tooth. '*Tzzza*! So the lion turned out to be a mouse. I guess tourists have to come all the way to discover that for themselves.'

'Yes.' I throw my jacket and bag on the chair.

'I cooked tomato sauce with basil and fresh chilli, but without meat, mind. We can eat it with pitta bread.'

'I'll see how she's doing first.'

She was lying on the sofa. When I placed my hand on her forehead she opened her eyes. Confusion followed by recognition then sadness. The cancer began as a tummy ache and the sound of my mother getting up at night several

12

times, swearing in the toilet and pacing around the house. She complained of acidity, kept burping as she chewed the fresh mint my grandmother had prescribed. I could tell that she was having a cramp by the paleness of her skin and the tightness of her lips. She began to fret over things: her marking, clipping the vine in the garden, sticking a simple dish of chicken and potato in the oven.

One morning my grandmother saw her pyjama trousers slip down. 'Fix that elastic, will you!'

'It's me, Mother. I am losing weight.'

That was it. My grandmother insisted on taking her to the doctor.

The doctor arranged something called a 'barium meal' and an X-ray immediately. It showed a tumour in the stomach. 'That would explain the dark stool and the anaemia.' And the regular trips to the hospital for chemotherapy began. She lay down on a sofa with a tube running into her chest, eyes closed and mouth open. She looked surprised. I held her hand as I listened to her breathing and the drip-drip of the white liquid that was supposed to kill the malignant cells. My grandmother counted her prayer beads and snivelled throughout the procedure. Then we supported her and shuffled back home. The milk seller said that it was grief, pure and simple – a dark fluid that went through your intestines and curdled like cheese. It fermented inside your guts.

Although my grandmother kept it clean, the house began to smell of vomit. I welcomed the early-morning trip to work. I walked by the girls' school, the grocer, chemist, rotisserie and clothes' shops to the public taxi stop. The mannequin was wearing fashionable tight leggings, a low-cut top and sparkling fake jewellery. Although my mother didn't allow me to wear a veil, like the other women of the neighbourhood, figure-hugging clothes were also banned. 'With an absent father, people might think you're a harlot.' So, caught in the middle, it was impossible to find the right outfit and leave the house without being reprimanded. Normally one parent dampens the temper of another, but I had to 'soar solo', as my teacher of English language would say.

I was able to put some of what I studied into practice at the hotel. I cleaned up the reception area and hid dusty dry flowers in the storage room. At first the owner found fault in everything I did. 'Look up when you're speaking to guests!' It was hard because my grandmother had cautioned me against looking men in the eye. I typed a letter in English, telling our guests what to do on arrival. 'That letter is too polite; they might end up not paying.' So I had to take out *please* and *thank you*. Then, just before printing it, I added *shukran*: thank you in Arabic, to spite him.

Our guests were mainly suited foreign men. 'What do they do?'

'They're journalists, arms' dealers and drug lords.'

14

'Really?'

'Yes. Most of them are.'

'Why do they come to Jordan? Not much happens here.'

'They come to unearth the truth.' He laughed, was gripped by a fit of coughing, then spat phlegm into his handkerchief.

She spat blood this morning. 'My mother is getting worse.'

'I am sorry, Najwa. May Allah cure her!'

She didn't believe in Allah for him to cure her. 'I have to take her to the doctor tomorrow for her chemo.'

'Fine, but you'll only be paid if your bum is on this seat.' He cackled.

He never missed an opportunity to be impolite.

The doctor said that there was no need for her to go to the clinic for treatment anymore. My grandmother gasped and covered her toothless gums with her hand. He prescribed some tablets that she could take at home. 'Just make her as comfortable as possible.' During the taxi journey, my mother seemed asleep and my grandmother kept wiping her tears with the end of her sleeve. The driver ogled me in the mirror; being the daughter of an absent father, they saw me as common land, without a fence or borders. I looked out at the setting sun and wondered who made that web you find yourself caught in. How did I end up here? Was there a way out? Can you soar solo?

My mother had changed; you wouldn't recognise her if

15

you bumped into her in the street. Most of her hair had fallen out and she had cracks by the corners of her mouth, ulcers spreading out of the arrow of her upper lips all the way to her nose and bruises on her biceps. She sat in bed, a skeleton with ashen skin and vacuous eyes, drifting off then floating back. We kept the radio next to her on. She woke up and listened sometimes. Once there was a reciting of the Qur'an before the Noon Prayer, which was normally transmitted from Mecca. She opened her eyes and when she heard the melancholic voice of the imam she flung the transistor against the wall and mentioned your name for the first time. 'Omar loved Allah, that's all.' It broke into pieces.

One night I couldn't sleep as I listened to her rasping. I got up and went to the sitting room where she liked to lie on the sofa. She looked at peace, as if all her battles were fought and won. She smiled when she saw me and patted the quilt. Cancer had reduced her to a few bones, rattling in a loose skin bag. She clasped my hand. 'I dried up like a date. After three years of absence, divorce can be granted easily.' She swallowed. 'The local doctor proposed, but I turned him down. He is still single. Don't be like me!' A fit of coughing. My grandmother got up and sat next to me. That was how it was: me in my pink Minnie Mouse pyjamas, my grandmother in her flannel nightie and my mother in her favourite kaftan. A rattle. She held my grandmother's shoulders. 'Thank you, Mother.' A wheeze. 'Najwa, sweetheart.' Dawn was breaking. We sat in the middle of the strips of light streaking through window bars. A snort, then she died. Her last words were, 'No Islamic funeral!'

Amman, January 1986

Busy morning. My wife is studying for her training course. She is up to her ears in teaching methodology and could not find Najwa's favourite toy, an electric Dalmatian that stands on its hind legs and wags its tail. She threw her notes on the bed and began crying. Najwa joined her mother. I put my jacket on and left the house of wailing women. Drowns in an inch of water. She gets frazzled, speechless as she tries to spit feathers out of her mouth. Needless to say she was as sweet as sugar when we first met in that public lecture on medieval love poetry.

Two buses to get to the hospital for Anatomy and Physiology II. The course explains the macroscopic and microscopic structure of the human body and the complexities and abstract nature of the organ system. What makes your heart stop – not a beautiful woman in a short skirt, as Hani would say. The man sitting next to me raised his arm to give the controller ten piasters. The smell of his sour sweat filled the air. A stink bomb. During his compulsory service, Hani was taught by a lisping sergeant about 'penetrating, exploding then burning grenades.'

The hospital is an old building at the top of a green hill. Green for Amman, that is: a few spindly pine trees stretching towards the light. A fug welcomed me when I entered through the main doors. The tart smell of unemptied chamber pots, vomit in corridors and blood. It must have been a devil of a night shift, something that is waiting for me when I graduate. My father said before he died,

17

'How can a man be a mumarida?' adding the /t/ of the feminine marker to the word to exclude his son. 'How can a man tend the sick, a woman?'

I answered him using a sentence I had heard on the radio, 'Nursing is an honest profession.' Words spoken for the benefit of fathers and brothers to convince them to allow their womenfolk to join the profession.

'My son! Wiping people's bottoms! Judgement day is nigh!'

I chose it simply because not many women are allowed to become nurses, whores in the eyes of many. Hani the joker said, 'Nurses have a bad reputation although most of the screwing is done by women teachers.'

The class is held at the back of the building. There is a staircase, then another, then Anatomy, written in large letters on the door. The hall has an adjacent morgue and a cadaver room with preserving tools. The teacher was miffed at having a full class and no corpse to dissect. 'We were promised a freshly dead man this morning, but the van is stuck in traffic in the outskirts of Amman. The only solution is to send two of you to the other hospital. A girl was stabbed by her brother and her family didn't want anything to do with the body.' Hani had never seen a naked girl before. He choked.

Two hours and a few cups of foul tea later, the body arrived. It was of a young woman, perhaps thirteen or fourteen, with multiple stab wounds. The teacher said, 'Obviously a victim of an honour killing.' He spat on the floor. 'Forensics will show that she was a virgin.'

18

We were not listening. Hani recited the lyrics of Olivia Newton-John's 'Xanadu' as if they were a sacred text. I remember when we first saw her in the film, singing about an impossible world, a land of ideals, of hope and love. A land that we could only dream of. Hani is obsessed with her. 'I wonder what blonde hair feels like.'

'It's just like dark hair.'

'How do you know? You've only run your hand over your wife's hair.'

'Leave my wife out of it!'

To our disappointment, the girl was dissected covered in a sheet. The lecturer waved the girl's heart in the air. It was small, encased in yellow fat and looked as if it was past its sell-by date. I took notes. 'Mammals have four-chambered hearts and double circulation. The left side handles only oxygenated blood, and the right side receives and pumps only deoxygenated blood. No mixing of the two kinds of blood.' Amazing that the good and bad blood are only separated by a thin wall! What would happen if it were punctured?

When we finished, Hani squeezed past me to chat up one of the female students. Light-skinned, of course, with folded eyelids like a reptile. He said, 'Good morning, Mademoiselle,' in the sweetest voice ever. And he didn't know French! She smiled. He shooed me away. I stood there next to him a tad longer than I should have, to spite him. He made a threatening gesture behind his back. When I walked away he ran his hand over his Miami Vice hairdo and sighed. He's been experimenting with his stubble to get it right. He grew it for two hours, half a day, two days, and then he came back with a result: seven hours and you have the perfect stayed-up-all-night look.

Back on the bus, I saw a number of police cars at the east gate of the university. A group of demonstrators carried placards saying, Democracy now! Free Palestine! Lower the Price of Commodities! The government has raised the price of everything: bread, fuel, rice. A warden diverted the traffic away from the protesters. They were surrounded by riot police, who are chosen from the toughest of tribes. No doubt there will be cracked skulls, broken thumbs and flayed skin. 'Yes, sir,' the driver said to the policeman and drove on out of his route. The journey will take much longer today.

We rarely go through the affluent west side. The sprinklers were swirling water over the lawns of large villas. There were drivers, gardeners, maids. Rumour has it that some of the gold in the glass entrance halls is real twenty-four carat. No wonder they have guards. What lies behind the privet hedges, the high metal gates, the closed shutters? Half-naked women? Men in tuxedos smoking cigars? Somebody was playing the saxophone, my favourite instrument. It caressed my very heart. The hoarseness and nostalgia of it. It tugged, it frisked and even licked.

Heading to town in a public taxi service, I looked at the lush gardens and lattice windows of the royal palaces on the opposite hill. Would they be swaying their hips to the sound of music? One day I found one of his records – Muhal

Richard Abrams, 'Blues Forever' – stuck between his books on nursing, in the cupboard. I took it out of its colourful sleeve, put it on the player, pressed *On* and listened to the beautiful tunes. The music carried me to unexplored mansions, cities, where people drank, smoked and danced cheek to cheek. I didn't hear the slam of the front door and her footsteps. She walked in on me – hair dishevelled, eyes smouldering and jaw jittering – pulled the needle, scratching the record, lifted it, dropped it on the floor and stepped all over it, destroying the disc and the round, colourful label.

I got out of the car, gathered my abaya and walked to the Bukharan market. I could barely understand his broken Arabic as I stood in the narrow alleyway of Amman's covered market surrounded by rugs, olive-wood camels, prayer beads, hands of Fatima, necklaces and bracelets. 'A secret conversation?' The immigrant seller, with his slanted eyes and pencil moustache, seemed certain that the inscribed words on the gold locket were in Pashto and had *confidential* and *whisper* in them. He tilted the locket towards the sun streaking through the market entrance. 'A fine piece. Where did you get it?'

The air was so laden with dust and the perfume of essential oils, I could hardly breathe. *A secret whisper.* What was he trying to tell me? Not used to mentioning him, I stammered, 'M-my father gave it to me.'

'Made in India or China, perhaps.'

My grandmother's yashmak, which I wore to disguise myself, kept slipping back and I pulled it down over my

21

hairline. My scalp was damp and sticky under the layers of cloth. I never wore a veil and was not used to its tightness under my chin. 'What is Pashto?'

'It is one of the languages spoken in the mountains of Asia.'

'How far?'

'Days and days of travel by land.'

'By air?'

'At least two flights.'

I unpinned the veil, loosened it, let some air in, tightened it again and checked that the face mask was in place.

'Can I tempt you with a cup of coffee?' He stroked his moustache with his index and middle fingers.

The seller either wanted to talk me into buying some of his souvenirs or make a pass at me. I stepped back. When tense, my right eyebrow arched up, a nervous tic that made me look like a villain. 'Thank you for your help.'

He sat behind the counter. '*Bir sey degil!*'

'*Bir sey degil!*' I repeated the foreign words.

'Don't mention it!' He smiled.

Clasping the locket, I wrapped the abaya around me, checked my purse and walked out of the shade of the market into the heat and hubbub of the city.

Taxis swerved tooting around buses, a truck full of breeze blocks was stuck in the traffic, street peddlers lined the pavements offering imitation watches and smuggled cigarettes, and the tamarind and carob drink peddler struck his cymbals

22

rhythmically. 'Quench your thirst!' The pedestrians, a mixture of farmers, natives and immigrant workers, surged forward under the colourful kaftans and scarves hung above our heads. Someone touched my bum and I leapt forward silently. If I resisted or shouted, people would find out about the violation and all the shame would be mine. I bit my tongue, something I am used to doing.

I stood on the pavement in the scorching heat opposite the Grand Mosque, which, despite its delicate appearance and pink-and-white stones, dominated the square. I had no option but to find my father. If my grandmother died, I would live alone in that house, something this city would not tolerate. Only women of ill repute live on their own without a male guardian. I would be pursued by predators, ostracised, and my door would be marked. If I'd had any choice, I would have let him go, for he was nothing to me, not even a memory.

Who could help me in this big city? The world was a maze and I didn't know where to enter it, how to navigate it and whether I would find a way out. If I asked the imam about my father's whereabouts, he might give me a clue or two. My late mother told me that before he abandoned us, my father went there every Friday to pray and returned home late. The call for Noon Prayer rose out of its two minarets and filled the market with its eternal sound. I crossed the busy road and stood under the arch of its main entrance, something my mother had cautioned me against. 'I lost my husband to religion, and I have no intention of offering my daughter on a plate to the nasty sheikhs. My name wouldn't be Raneen if I allowed that!' Her name was Raneen and she buzzed and chattered. The toothless mosque attendant soaked the mop in the bucket full of water, dark with grime, wrung it out, then wiped the floor. Steam rose as soon as it touched the hot marble. He stopped and gawped when he saw me leaning against the gate. 'What do you want?'

'I would like to see the imam.' My eyes met his.

He wagged his finger. 'Shoo! It's prayer time. No women, chit-chat or nonsense.'

'Please.'

'Shoo!' He raised the mop.

This mission was going to be harder than I thought.

I rushed to the gold market, past the juice kiosk, the cassette stand and the trinkets shop. The floor was swept then sprinkled with water to cool the air in its alleyways. The necklaces dangling in the show windows glinted in the sun. They were pure, high in carat and dark. If I were like other girls I would be shopping for a set with my future husband, not skulking like a thief. My grandmother had advised me to keep checking for nosy hags, relatives with wagging tongues and neighbourhood gossips. 'No one must find out that we've resorted to selling our assets.' I chose a shop at the end of the row and pushed the glass door open. When the air-conditioned draught hit my muslin-covered face, I shuddered.

24

The trousers, shoes and hair of the man behind the counter shone in the electric spotlights. Spending endless hours cooped up in this shop, his skin was as pale as dough. I lay our gold on the glass display box: my grandmother's Ottoman coins and *jhumka* earrings, my mother's set, my two rings and pendant with turquoise beads. I fidgeted, shifting my weight from one foot to the other. If anyone saw me sell the family's jewellery, there would be endless trouble. He ran his pasty fingers over our heirlooms then weighed them, jotted down a few notes, keyed in some figures on the calculator. 'I'll give you five thousand dinars.'

My grandmother had sucked her last tooth, a gesture that sometimes meant no and at other times wonderment, when she told me, 'You must haggle with the greedy usurers.'

'Ten thousand or nothing!' I said. 'Take it or leave it!'

He deliberated with his partner, who was in the back, probably fixing broken gold hearts and Allah necklaces. 'Six thousand dinars.'

'Ten thousand.' I gathered the jewellery and began walking out, as I had been instructed by my grandmother. She'd said that it was probably worth twenty thousand.

When I was by the door, he called out, 'Nine thousand dinars, cash on the table.'

I shook my head. Being stupid and stubborn, I gripped the door handle, about to leave.

He rolled the banknotes and tied them with a rubber band.

The muscle in my right cheek twitched.

I went back, dropped the jewellery on the counter and slipped the money into the hidden pocket of the abaya, before fixing the yashmak and heading out into the midday heat.

I walked through the hustle and bustle of the capital by the vegetable market, the Roman pool where nymphs used to swim, the shop that sells books on aliens and jinn, by the second-hand mobile stands and the amphitheatre up the hill to save the thirty piasters public cars charged per passenger. If I was going to find my father, I needed every penny.

The smell of bread preceded the sight of the long queue at the bakery. Dough kneaders dusted with flour sat on the platform in their underpants smoking. My grandmother told me that my father would come home at lunchtime carrying a sack full of flat bread, get a clean towel out, spread the loaves on it and leave them to cool down. The aroma lingered in our small kitchen. Did he give me a piece of bread to chew on or was my memory playing tricks on me? Did he ever hold me? Was I conceived by mistake or design? Did my parents want me?

A man stopped his car next to me. 'Psst! Psst! Come here!'

He thought I was a prostitute in disguise. Some wore the Islamic dress to hide their identity. 'Just wait there!' I said. 'Police!'

'Your loss!' He pressed down on the accelerator and raced away.

People thought that I belonged to everybody because my father was not around to protect me. I stood panting at the top of the steep hill. On the opposite hill, houses were stacked on top of each other like caardboard boxes. Who lived in them? Were they proper families: fathers, mothers, children and perhaps grandfathers or grandmothers? Were they happy? I wiped the sweat off my face with my sleeve and trudged back home.

'Hello, Grandma!' She was sitting in the garden, snipping parsley, her grey hair gathered in a scarf, her eyes beady, face wrinkled and fingers bent with arthritis. I took off the muslin yashmak and the abaya instantly and flung them on the floor. 'How do veiled women function under those? Honestly! And the heat is overbearing.'

She sucked her last tooth and pushed up her bifocals. 'How much?'

I sat down next to her and handed her the money. 'Nine thousand.'

'Good girl!'

'One has to learn to soar solo,' I said in English, repeating what the teacher had said.

'"Sooor soooloo"? What does that mean?' She offered me an extra-sweet mint-flavoured tea.

I had a sip then translated the sentence.

'Flowery words, then life knocks you.'

'Grandma!'

'If your mother was alive, she wouldn't have approved.' She coughed and pushed her glasses up.

The tin box full of photos was next to her as usual. She

27

opened it, took out a photo of her only daughter when she was young – my age, perhaps – raised it up and inspected it. 'You look like her, Najwa.'

She had dark curly hair, which was wrapped with a pink-and-white striped scarf, perfect skin, arched brows, large brown eyes, a nose with a slight tilt and an arrow-shaped upper lip and a full lower one. She was wearing the earrings I had just sold. I looked away.

My grandmother ran her fingers over it. 'I have lost her and now I will . . .' Her chin quivered.

'I could stay.' Her hand was swollen and stiff in mine.

'No, you must go and look for your father. The past might make you whole.'

'What about you?'

'I'll not last long. You cannot live in this house on your own after I am gone. What would people say?'

'But . . .'

'If you end up on your own in this house, it will be so shameful. Only loose women, *'ahirat*, live alone. You belong with your father.'

I dreamt about him walking through that door, kneeling down and kissing my hair, eyes, cheeks, hands. 'Forgive me for leaving you behind.' He stroked me, sniffed my neck and held me tight.

'What if he does not want to see me, have anything to do with me?'

She put my mother's photo back in the box and spread the parsley leaves in the tray. 'Then his heart is made of flint.'

28

Amman, March 1986

My daughter, Najwa – olive-skinned, brown-eyed and nimble – toddles here and there. A gap between her front teeth waters down her beauty, makes her unique. When her mother gave birth to her and she opened her eyes, I saw the world through them. The dayah *cleaned her then wrapped her in a swaddling blanket, pinned the gold hand of Fatima to her chest, a gift from her dead grandfather. I was too apprehensive to hold her.*

The toothless dayah *said, 'You must hold her! Say the azan in her ear.'*

She was a sparrow in my arms: warm, her ribcage small, heart throbbing. I whispered in her ear.

She is soft and malleable, unlike her mother. I have a good wife, who cooks, cleans, takes care of Najwa, studies for her exam. But she gets flustered sometimes, uptight, and starts dropping pots, spoons, slamming doors. And when this happens I pray for her ice to melt, for her shoulders to unknot, her mouth to untwist itself. When she is angry I find her unattractive like an ugly rock formation. Impenetrable!

So I escape her grip to Xanadu whenever possible. Hani and I started our night of conviviality at the local rotisserie, where chickens, rubbed with spices and thyme and mounted on the spit, revolve in front of the grill. The fat dripped and sizzled on the hot tin. It was a cold night. I stretched my hands over the fire and filled

29

my nostrils with the aroma of richly cooked food. Hani was paying tonight because his boss at the garage had finally given him his wages.

We sat on the wall overlooking Amman and the royal palaces sprawled at the top of the opposite hill. Oblivious to the cars hooting, shops closing and the call to prayer, we ate and drank, dangling our feet. Hani bought himself a whole chicken with potato wedges and garlic dip. He grabbed it with both hands, tore it to pieces and began eating, fat running down his fingers. Before I had a sip of the fizzy drink I had bought, he pushed it away and gave me a brown bag. It had a beer bottle in it.

'We cannot drink here, in our neighbourhood.'

'Yes, we can. We can drink anywhere.'

'If we get spotted, we will become pariahs.'

'I want to get so drunk that that old hag buying nuts over there turns into Brigitte Bardot.'

I looked behind me to see if anyone was watching, taking notes, reporting straight back to God, then had a swig. The beer was sweet and sour.

'You know, Omar, when I get drunk I start imagining things: spiders crawling on my scalp, their legs fine and hairy. Perhaps they mix this shit with bleach or arsenic.' He wiped his mouth with his arm.

'I don't see things, but I suddenly panic as if I have been caught out. Perhaps I was a murderer in my previous life. I think I am being watched all the time.'

'That is because you are being watched!'

30

'I keep washing myself, scrubbing my skin, trying to be pure.'

'It can only be achieved in death.'

The beer bottle was finished. He dropped it in a garbage barrel and rubbed his hands on his flared trousers. His Afro was like a black fez above his head.

We decided to go to the Privé in west Amman. Hani shrugged off my feeble objection and hailed a taxi. It is a long ride from the east, the poor side, where the riff-raff like us live, all the way to the affluent west side. Hani was in a good mood. He spoke about his love of American women: lean, toasted like wholewheat bread, legs long and up to their ears. He wants to get married to one of them and leave this country forever. It will be his ticket out, his deliverance from the drudgery and ugliness. He was sure that he would find one in a boîte de nuit. Western women are always in nightclubs.

It was dark inside the club and I could barely see. A whiff of cigarette smoke, perfume and sweat hits you when you enter. Loud music: 'Girls Just Want To Have Fun'. And there was uncovered flesh, yards of it, and women with ample hips swaying on the dance floor. I had died and gone to Muslim paradise, where damsels and houris reclined on sofas. One of them came towards me and asked me to dance. Her darkness was hidden behind a white mask of make-up, an aquamarine circle around her eyes. I wanted to say no, that I was married, and looked to Hani for support. He was nowhere to be seen. I gingerly moved to the dance floor. She bent her elbows and dug them into my chest to keep me at a decent distance from her. That is slow dancing local style. Full-frontal contact is not allowed.

31

Hani was homing in on a tall blonde, a foreigner perhaps, easier; no elbows dug in his ribcage. He tucked his fringe behind his ear, wiped his hands against his shirt and held her hand carefully, as if she were made of porcelain. If she were American, she would be precious. She wrapped her arms around his neck and moved closer. The lucky bastard!

The music was good. I love The Police's 'Every Breath You Take', especially the soft tunes at the beginning. Rhythmic movement of bodies. Breath on your face. Repeating the lyrics in unison. And suddenly I felt tired. Hani had disappeared. The made-up face looked distorted close up. My nerve ends were pop-popping. I excused myself and left.

Dawn was breaking over Amman. The sky was streaked with warm hues of red. I breathed in the clean air and walked down the valley eastwards. To cross three hills on foot was crazy, but I would sober up. I walked by a deserted petrol station, a few old stores and a church. When I looked up, there was the citadel, its columns still standing. Seven thousand years of history. It looked eerie in the first light. Those who lived in it – multiplied, celebrated and grieved, buried babies in jars under the tiles – are no more. The breeze carried their cries and laughter to my ears. Perhaps there is something beyond this soil and sperm. Perhaps we are little islands floating on fresh water endlessly, eternally.

It was five o'clock in the morning when I finally arrived home. I took off my clothes in the sitting room and tiptoed to the bedroom. My mother-in-law was snoring. Thank God my wife, the interior minister, was asleep, her chest rising and falling. With my mental condition as it was, I couldn't handle an inquisition. If she asked me where I'd been and whether I'd been drinking, I would break down, or leave forever, start my wandering years, follow my nomadic heart.

I picked up my notebook and began writing. She often asks me why I keep scribbling, which is what it really is. I write to hold on to the present, tie it down before it becomes past, navigate through the maze of my life, understand where I am at, see the larger picture, where the forest begins and ends, so to speak. Keeping a diary is the act of a small man – poor, subjugated, powerless. I spill ink and dreams on the page. Prophet Mohammed said, 'When you see an evil act you have to stop it with your hand. If you can't, then at least speak out against it with your tongue. If you can't, then at least resist it in your heart. And this is the weakest of faith.'

Bad morning. Splitting headache, sulking wife, screaming baby and an old woman snivelling in the kitchen. How did I find myself here? Me – the man who wanted to walk around the world? On foot, no less. Since I read 'Around the World in Eighty Days', I wanted to be Passepartout, a traveller with little luggage, hopping from one train to another, a Thomas Cook, an Ibn Battuta. Where is Xanadu?

I secured the rubber band around my notebook and went to the kitchen. Perhaps I could comfort Najwa, stop her crying.

Looking through the window, I wondered what tribes, animals and trees grew beyond the horizon. I'd never seen a river, a lake or a large pool full of fresh water, its surface reflecting the stars, dotting the night sky. My grandmother said that knowledge might set you free or imprison you forever. The hills that besiege us looked deserted now the trains had stopped travelling to Damascus. Even the boys, who used to play on the arid land, had disappeared. When I was a child I used to be terrified of the sorceress who lived there. Who was she and how come she lived on her own up there? What if she decided to walk out of her hut, cross the valley and come after us? Her house disappeared and was replaced by blocks of flats rising asymmetrically towards the sky. Some of the buildings were still unfinished and the bare iron bars looked like hair on a head.

The view of the hills took me back to the day when the past unfurled like a roll of fabric. A few weeks after the death of my mother, the imposer of rules and regulations, I had been free to search the house for clues, photos, documents – anything that would help me construct a father. I climbed up to the loft, switched on the light, dusted the suitcase and unzipped it. My father's prayer shirt was at the top. With trembling fingers I held it up and had a sniff. A faint, pleasant scent – musk or sandalwood, perhaps – mingled with your natural smell. I hugged it and wrapped the sleeves around me. You used to hold me tight and fling me up in the air. Your hands were large, your fingers strong around my waist.

There was an unopened box of chocolates with a red ribbon tied in a neat diagonal bow and a Turkish tassel for a handle. You wouldn't see this kind of packaging these days in the shops of humble east Amman. The expiry date was October 1986, when I was three. That was the year my father had abandoned us. I opened it gingerly. Each chocolate was wrapped in a different coloured cellophane paper: orange sensation, caramel caress, dreamy fudge and almond crunch. Did my father give them to my mother? I unwrapped one and it crumbled in my hand, a mixture of dry fat and dead white worms. The chocolates were past their expiry date, but my mother had kept them, clinging to a memory until it had gone sour.

The shoebox was full of black and white photos of him. I held one portrait, ran my fingers over his moustache and beard, traced the large eyes and the full lips. My dad! There were photos of him standing by an old car with his friends. He was clean-shaven then, with long curly hair, parted almost in the middle, and sideburns. There was a stern photo of him with a dedication on the back: *To Najwa, lest she forget!* Another showed him behind a wooden desk with his head down in a large class. The scribble on the back said, *Modern Languages Centre, Mango Market, King Faisal Street, 1984.* Then him with a young man in a tight shirt, with Afro hair, bushy moustache and flared trousers: *To my dear friend Omar, my partner in crime. With my love and high esteem. Hani.* Him standing in a hospital by a patient's bed. My grandmother told me that he studied nursing at college and went on to destroy lives rather than heal them.

I found a few pieces of jewellery in a velvet bag. The foreign words inscribed on the heart-shaped locket and the embossed floral surround were uneven against my palm. I clicked it open. Inside, a few emerald-green silk threads, arranged like an eight-pointed star, were held under the clear sheet of resin. The pendant was a string of letters in some language, similar to a name or script necklace. There was a gold ring at the bottom of the bag. I tried it on and it fitted my thumb. The names of my parents and their wedding date, May 1981, were engraved on the gold. Muslim men must never wear fineries, like gold or silk, and must remain stoic. He wore gold in 1981, a sure sign that he was not a strict Muslim. He took his wedding ring off, then left unadorned. What happened to him between 1981 and 1986? What changed him from a secular student of nursing to someone else, perhaps heartless? In four years, he turned from a normal father and a husband into a vagabond. Was he a mercenary?

I put the jewellery bag and his portrait photo into my pocket, slid his wedding ring on to my thumb, put everything back where it was, zipped up the suitcase and climbed down all the way from the past to the present.

The aroma of rich food filled the house. My grandmother was cooking my favourite dish: aubergine and lamb stew.

'Najwa, where have you been? I wanted you to peel the garlic for me.'

'Grandma, I have to go to the mosque. Do you think they'll let me in?'

'Not in a short-sleeved top, your hair uncovered.'

I took my grandmother's veil, tied it around my head, draped her loose abaya over my shoulders and ran out.

'Najwa! The mosque is under surveillance!'

It was a humble 1940s building by the roadside with an open metal gate, glass windows and a minaret lined with green neon lights. Worshippers flooded out after the Noon Prayer. I stood in the cool shade of the building, panting. One of the men pointed at me. 'What does she want?'

The mosque attendant, who knew all the people of the neighbourhood, recognised me, put on his slippers and came out. 'What can I do for you?'

I could see a sliver of an ornate rug through the door. 'I want to see the imam, please.'

'I'll see what I can do.' He shuffled away.

The male worshippers sized me up as I stood on the pavement shifting my weight from one foot to the other. Some sneered, others made snide remarks and some found my presence outside the gate, a space reserved for males and beggars, offensive. I stayed put, despite the tic in my right cheek.

The attendant came back, rearranged his kaffiyeh headdress and ushered me to a side door. He opened it and asked me to enter. I took off my shoes and placed the sole of my foot gingerly on the threshold of a mosque for the first time, then crossed it. The inside was humble: carpeted floors, some bookcases, a few plastic chairs. It was like the clinic of the only doctor in the neighbourhood, the one who had spent years chasing after my late mother. He led me down a dimly lit corridor to one of the offices at the back. Someone roared a 'Come in!' when he knocked.

The imam sat behind a desk with a glass top, his Qur'an open on a rest, his prayer beads in a bowl next to an old dial phone. He waved me in and asked me to sit down. The white kaffiyeh hid most of his raven hair, and his eyes were intense, lips purple and his beard groomed and anointed. He lowered his gaze and counted his prayer beads. Allah permitted the first glance, but the second look at a strange woman's face was a sin and the imam tried hard to abide. 'What can I do for you? If you are after financial help, our *zakat* money is finished. We have to wait for doers-of-good to donate some more.' There were no windows in the room and I could smell the dust gathered in the corners.

My grandmother advised me to approach the subject gently. 'Thank you for agreeing to see me, imam. I assure you I am not after money. What I need is your help.'

'Allah willing, I will be able to offer it to you.'

I stuck my hand in the hidden pocket of the abaya, pulled my father's photo out and placed it on the desk in front of him. 'I am looking for my father.'

38

He stood up. 'You're Omar Rahman's daughter. Welcome! Welcome! What an honour!'

'I need to find him, revered imam. Do you know where he is?'

'My daughter,' he said, although, at twenty-seven, I was too old to be his daughter, 'no one knows his whereabouts. He was a disciple of Sheikh Muhammad, a protégé of Sheikh Azzam. They all left the country.'

'Sheikh Muhammad? Sheikh Azzam?'

He hid his astonishment. 'When the Soviet Union invaded Afghanistan in 1979, Sheikh Azzam, Allah bless his soul, issued a fatwa declaring that both the Afghan and Palestinian struggles were jihads, holy wars.'

'And?'

'Sheikh Muhammad, here, spread his message. Your father spent hours debating Azzam's fatwa with Sheikh Muhammad. Many young men decided to join.'

'Join what?'

'Global jihad, of course. They were given salaries, plane tickets and accommodation at the other end.'

'Where?'

The imam hesitated, stopped counting the prayer beads, picked up the telephone receiver then put it down.

'I need to find him. It's urgent.' I clasped my hands and put them in my lap.

'The only way forward is to talk to his friend Hani's family. Rumour has it that he was with him when he was martyred. They live just around the corner, past the spice shop.'

'His friend Hani is dead?'

'Yes, he died. May Allah bless his soul!'

'Thank you so much for your help.'

He raised his curled lashes and looked at me. A sinful second glance! 'Please accept my condolences for the death of your mother. May Allah's paradise be her final abode!'

I wasn't sure she would have liked that. I nodded.

'Do you still go to college?'

'I took time out to take care of my mother.' The perfume of camphor essential oils was overpowering.

'Will you go back? What are you studying?' I could hear the click-click of sandalwood prayer beads knocking against each other.

I cleared my voice. 'Grateful to you, imam. Must go now.' I stretched out my hand.

The imam recoiled and pressed his hand against his chest. A simple gesture, which meant *I consider your flesh a temptation and any contact with it is forbidden.*

I walked out of the cool shade into the glare of the hot sun. The fine hair at the nape of my neck stood up. I was being watched. I wrapped the abaya round me and rushed past the barber, grocer, the shoe-repair kiosk and the spice shop, and turned right up the hill. I counted one, two, three houses and stood in front of an iron gate, freshly painted black. The aroma of chicken and rice filled the air. It was lunch hour and people never visited each other between one and three o'clock. I was about to press the bell then hesitated. Perhaps they started their siesta early. I decided to go back home for some lunch and come back in the afternoon.

Amman, May 1986

Hani the rascal has been acting weird lately. He has been disappearing on Sunday and Tuesday nights instead of joining me at the local café for a game of cards and a few hubbly-bubbly puffs. Perhaps I could catch him and invite him out for some lamb kebabs. Needless to say there will be hell to pay later on. My wife will get worked up and then sulk. The only remedy is to ignore her for a few days and do what I please, then bring her chocolates or fruit leather. 'You cannot bribe me,' she will say as she chews on an apricot sheet, her favourite.

I have looked for Hani at the rotisserie, the barber, the nut seller, the café, even the mosque, and cannot find him. He normally leaves me a message at the barber's to tell me about his plans. Not today. Is he seeing a married woman? Returned home early to have my mother-in-law's signature dish: bulgar wheat with ground lamb, rolled into rissoles then fried.

It's hot and my back is wet with sweat. Najwa is ill and off her food. I put cold pads on her forehead, but her temperature is still

41

high. Her cheeks glow in the light of the setting sun. She shivers and coughs, bringing up phlegm, green in colour. My wife mashed a banana and mixed it with orange juice, but she wouldn't eat, drink or pass urine. Her breathing is shallow and rapid. The doctor has prescribed liquid antibiotics, but she resists dripping them into her mouth. She wheezes into the night.

I have convinced my wife to go to bed for a couple of hours, promising to keep an eye on Najwa. Her cheeks are red. I took her top off and placed my hands around her ribs. She seemed so small. And love raced through me, warming my limbs like a hot shower. I kissed the top of her head.

Sitting by her bed, I was reading about acute bronchitis in Medical-Surgical Nursing: 'Antibiotics are not usually advised if you are normally in good health. Your immune system can usually clear the infection. Antibiotics do not kill viruses. Even if a bacterium is the cause, antibiotics usually do little to speed up recovery of an acute bronchitis.' Yet the local doctor hands them out like candy and my wife gives them to my daughter whenever she sneezes. She thinks she is always right.

While Najwa was ill, I neglected my friend Hani. Finally, weeks later, we arranged to meet in a downtown café called Old Amman, overlooking the Roman citadel at the top of the hill. Concerned about others listening to our conversation, we decided to sit outside on the 1930s balcony with its delicate iron railing, sipping cinnamon-flavoured tea and smoking a hubbly bubbly. Hani pointed at the arched entrance. 'The beginning of a tunnel *connecting the castle with the amphitheatre. A safe passage for the rulers.'*

He seemed different; his skin was darker and his eyes shifted between the street, the hills and the dog barking under the fig tree at the back of the café.

'I haven't seen you for a long time. Where have you been hiding?'

'Hiding!'

'Is it a married woman? A street hooker? A belly dancer in a club?'

'No.'

'Did you sleep with that American woman?'

'Yes. We went to a cheap downtown hotel. She helped me out of my clothes and kissed me all over but when my dream came true, I couldn't rise to the challenge.'

'You couldn't raise the Arab flag? You're a disgrace!'

'It was midday when I finally did her. But I felt so dirty afterwards I scoured my skin with a scrubbing sponge and washing powder. How do you purify yourself?'

'So you're no longer a virgin.'

'No.'

'Why do you look so sad? Did she do the disappearing act on you?'

'No. She wanted more and I broke it off.'

'What? Are you insane?'

The fig tree leaves rustled. He almost jumped.

'Why do you look so glum?'

'I wish I could tell you.'

'Are you in trouble with the police?'

'I will be.'

The breeze was gentle on our faces and the city was winding down. Fewer horns being blown frantically.

Hani told me that after his sexual adventure, he felt so guilty he joined a study circle that met regularly next to the Grand Mosque. 'It is an Islamic political organisation, established in 1953. It works at all levels of society to restore the Islamic way of life under the umbrella of the caliphate.'

'Khilafah? Sounds so medieval!'

Hani was upset. 'Our political aim is the re-establishment of the Islamic caliphate as a state – having an elected and accountable ruler, an independent judiciary.'

I hadn't heard ruler and accountable in one sentence before, so I got jittery. I could see the police wandering about between the columns of the forum. 'You're joking, right?'

'No; the role of the caliph is to serve the masses, governing them with justice.'

Another word I hadn't heard lately: justice. Hani needed to lower his voice. The place was teeming with secret police. Perhaps because he is single, he is reckless. I, on the other hand, am married with responsibilities and a daughter to feed. I told Hani what he already knew. 'You're dreaming. This is far out. You're going to establish a caliphate in this day and age. How?'

Hani began spewing a pre-rehearsed argument. He spoke about using logic to prove the existence of Allah.

'An atheist asked Imam Abu Hanifa if Allah really exists. "Forget it! At the moment I am busy thinking about this ship. There is no one to steer it, yet it traverses big waves on the oceans; it stops at the locations that it is supposed to stop at; it continues in the direction that it is supposed to head. This ship has no captain and no one planning its trips."

'The atheist who posed the question interrupted, "How can any intelligent person think that something like this is possible?"

'Imam Abu Hanifa said, "I feel sorry for you! You cannot imagine one ship running without a captain, yet you think that no one looks after or owns this whole world, which runs precisely."

'Hearing the reply, the atheist was left speechless. He finally found the truth and proclaimed Islam.'

I was dumbfounded. Hani the secular sounded like the imam of the Martyr's Mosque. He spewed out nonsense for hours.

My grandmother was standing by the gate looking at the alleyway. She was relieved to see me. 'You're late. I want to serve lunch.'

I took off the veil and the abaya and flung them on the sofa, there where my mother used to writhe in agony.

'I made you lemon and mint sherbet. It's in the fridge.'

The kitchen was a mess, but the table in the middle was clean and set.

'In the name of Allah,' my grandmother said and began serving the rice and stew.

I spooned some up and ate. The lamb was cooked to perfection and it fell apart when I poked it with the fork. 'Bless your hands, Grandma!'

'Was your visit to the mosque useful?'

'Yes; the imam said that my father went away with his friend Hani.' I gulped down the food. 'I'll go to see his family this afternoon.'

'Not before three o'clock and not before you have some sherbet. I made it especially for you.'

'Of course.' I kissed her arthritic fingers.

'And don't speak with your mouth full!'

I stood outside Hani's family's house, hair tied, back straight and uncomfortable in one of my mother's suits. The gate was open so I walked through an empty yard to the house in the middle. There were no flowers in the beds, no fountain, no pots full of begonia. Weeds sprang from the cracks between the concrete walls and the ground. I knocked on the door and heard a feeble, 'Come in!'

I went into a dark room with built-in seats. A grey-haired woman reclined on one of them. She looked up.

'Peace be upon you!'

'Who are you? Are you a gypsy beggar?'

'No. I am Najwa.'

She stuck her finger in her ear and shook it. 'Najwa?'

'Omar Rahman's daughter.'

She knocked her head against the wall, rubbed it, got up

46

and rushed to the kitchen. 'Abu-Hani! Guess who is in our house? Omar Rahman's daughter!'

Hani's father shuffled in, fixed his white kaffiyeh and said, '*Ahlan*! Welcome to my house! You brought light and gladness to this darkness.' He urged me to sit down.

The woman kissed me on both cheeks.

'Are you Hani's mother?'

'Yes, I am the martyr's mother.'

'Long life to you and your children!'

My grandmother advised me to fill my mouth with sugar to sweeten the words. 'I hope that you're in good health and spirits.'

'Unfortunately we are in good health, but our spirits . . .'

Hani's father said, 'Thanks be to Allah. Whatever He decrees, we accept.'

'I heard about your loss. I am sorry.'

'Thank you!'

'What can we do for you?'

'I am here to ask you about my father.'

'Your father is the most honourable of men. He carried my son over his shoulder for miles. Hani – my precious, my heart, my eyesight – died in his arms.'

'Died in his arms? Where?'

'In Mazar.'

'When?'

'Six years ago.'

She stood up, went to the kitchen and came back with tea and a photo of Hani and my father standing in the middle of

47

a field of poppies, the mountains high behind them. His head was covered with a black shawl, his beard was bushy and he looked tall and thin in a tunic and loose trousers.

'This is the shalwar kameez of the Taliban,' Hani's father said.

You were covered with dust and looked rugged and weather-beaten. 'He can't be my dad.'

'It's your father. He is a *mujahid*.'

'A mujahid?'

'Yes; he is fighting for Allah.'

'Fighting for Allah.'

'He's one of the soldiers of Islam.'

'One of the soldiers of Islam!' I parroted.

The house smelt of dust and decay. I wanted to leave, but I fixed my feet to the ground and had another sip of the extra-sweet tea. They told me that Hani had decided to go to Afghanistan and managed to convince my father to join him. They went to Peshawar. Hani's parents didn't know much. The rest was hearsay. After the massacre in the mountains of Afghanistan, my father, who was a medic, carried Hani all the way to the nearest hospital. He died on the way. My father pressed his intestines back into the cavity of his belly. He was clean. There was no blood. Martyrs die clean and fragrant. After that, no one had heard from my father.

'Perhaps he's in the caves of Tora Bora with Sheikh Osama,' Hani's father said.

They didn't know my father's whereabouts, but they agreed to give me a copy of the photo. 'I have so many hanging around the house.'

I shook Hani's father's hand, kissed his mother and left.

Clasping the photo, I went to the local internet café, a space out of bounds for chaste women. Only men went there, to sit in front of the computer screens, cracking roasted watermelon seeds, smoking hubbly bubbly and searching for sites of ill repute. If I walked in, they would think that I was looking for chance encounters. Breaking the rules of the community was easy. One foot after another and I was right in the middle of that cloud of smoke and nicotine. I asked for a two-dinar pass and sat down. I keyed in *Mazar* and the search engine packed up.

'There are certain words that make the system go doolally,' the owner said and typed in *cache*. The following appeared on the screen:

Mazar-e-Sharif مزار شريف is the fourth largest city of Afghanistan. It means 'Noble Shrine', a reference to the large blue-tiled sanctuary and mosque in the centre of the city known as the Shrine of Hazrat Ali or the Blue Mosque.

When I keyed in *Mazar Taliban war*, the screen went blank, but before it did I was able to read, *Afghan massacre. The convoy of death.*

49

The cyber café attendant said, 'Now the system has truly crashed. Certain words make the censor jittery. OK, *shabab*! You can go home now. The server is down.'

Suddenly all the men turned and ogled me. I buttoned up my mother's jacket and walked out, tainted and with little information on Mazar-e-Sharif.

My grandmother was sitting in the garden in what used to be my mother's chair, her head in her hands, crying.

I wrapped my arms around her.

'She didn't have much life. Did she?'

'I know, Grandma! But God has retrieved his deposit.' A phrase I had heard our religious neighbour use.

'He deposited her here and made her suffer.' She wiped the tears with the end of her scarf.

'Don't cry, Grandma!'

'And now you're leaving.' She clasped my hand with her bent thumb and forefinger.

'I could stay.'

She put her glasses on. 'No, sweetheart, you must find your father.'

That night, I took the photos out of my bag, studied the one Hani's mother had given me and compared it to the one of you when you were young and dashing. That man with grey hair, wrinkled skin, rough hands was supposed to be you. Impossible! There was no resemblance between the weather-beaten older man and the young one with curly hair, fringe tucked behind his ear and flared trousers. The mountains behind you were soaring and higher than the hills surrounding us here, and the plain was covered with bright coloured poppies. You were wrapped in a long shawl. A young girl was playing behind you in the distance. Was it cold? Who was the young girl? And why was Hani holding a rifle but you were unarmed?

In the morning, I kissed my grandmother's hand and took a taxi to the Identity and Passport Service in the west side. The man by the gate asked, 'Why are you here alone?'

'I have no male relatives.'

He sized me up. 'I don't believe you. Did you grow out of a tree?'

'My father is away, my mother is dead and my grandmother is too old to leave the house.'

He let me in. It took three hours to get to the front of the queue and hold the attention of the civil servant in charge of issuing passports. My grandmother had insisted that I wear my mother's best teaching suit and the cheap material absorbed rather than deflected the heat. The form I handed him was damp.

'Are you married? If you are I need your husband's permission.'

'No, I am not married.' I wrung my hands.

'Go over there and write a statement pledging that you are single! Don't forget the stamps.'

I wrote it, signed it, stuck the postal stamps on it, then joined the queue again.

51

He fingered his trimmed moustache. 'Not many women come here on their own like that to get their passport issued.'

I bit my lower lip and handed him the papers. My grandmother had told me to keep quiet about my father. '*If they find out that you intend to travel to Pakistan, you'll be in trouble.*'

'My father is away and my mother is dead.'

He hesitated, stamped it and passed it. 'A few minutes and your passport will be ready.'

I stood in a narrow street in the heat, holding my first passport. The sun was in the middle of the sky. The gold script on its green leather glinted and suddenly, as if by magic, the country became larger than our house, garden and my college. I could cross its borders, take a taxi for hours or board a plane. Under the watchful eye of the Passport Service guards, I went to the nearest kiosk and bought a bottle of fizzy drink to celebrate. My grandmother told me that Muslim men and women were not supposed to eat in public. They were discredited and their testimony would not be accepted in court. I unscrewed the top and drank. Its coldness and sweetness was so refreshing. Men were stealing glances at me. The journey hadn't started yet and three rules were broken already: I'd been into a male-only internet café, got a passport without my male guardian's permission and drunk in public. The man minding the kiosk smiled. '*Sahtain!* To your health! Did you enjoy that?'

I hailed a taxi.

The Pakistani embassy was a humble white stone and red brick building across the street from a church. I entered, filled in the form, paid the fee and joined the queue. Our religious neighbour had told us that it was really difficult to get a visa to Pakistan nowadays. Her son had tried several times and was turned down. 'They're afraid that the young men might end up in training camps.'

An attractive man, with dusky skin and dark, glistening hair, looked up. He spoke in English. 'Why do you want to go to Pakistan?'

On the form, I put tourism as the reason for the visit. To look for the father I never had.

'What is the reason for your visit?' he said impatiently.

Behind my father in the photograph there were so many peaks against the sky. 'The mountains.'

He smiled. 'The second highest mountain in the world is in Pakistan. Don't tell me you're going to climb it!'

'I have to climb it.' My English language lessons began when I was eleven, plus a few extra classes at college. I understood him perfectly.

'Do you know anyone there?'

'No. I am studying tourism. It be good for me.'

He stamped a three-month visa on my brand new passport.

When I got back home, the house was quiet. There was no chit-chat, songs about small cafés or weeping. I tiptoed into the bedroom and there was my grandmother, in her white pilgrimage clothes, lying in bed with her eyes closed. She had saved up to have the attire made, but she never made it to Mecca. My mother wouldn't give her the money to go. The white sheets covered her like a shroud. Was she dead? I put my palm against her mouth. She was breathing.

I called her, the way my mother used to: 'Mama Zainab, are you all right?'

She opened her eyes. 'Am I still alive?'

'Yes, Grandma!' I pulled up the white garment to cover her neck.

'What a shame! I did my ablutions this morning and wore my *ihram* clothes, hoping that Allah would have mercy on me and take me away.'

'Don't say such things!'

She pulled her veil down. Her grey hair was so thin it barely covered her scalp, which was red and blotchy. 'He denied me death.'

'Grandma! You cannot choose the timing of your departure.'

'How could my young daughter die before me? It's not natural.' She slipped in her partial dentures and bit.

'Mama Zainab! I brought you some Turkish delights. The ones flavoured with rose water.'

She sat up in bed. 'Stop calling me "Mama Zainab"! You're not my late daughter!'

'OK, Grandma, *habibti*! How about a cup of tea with fresh mint?' I slipped her scarf back and tucked the thinning strands of hair under it.

She sat up. 'I'd better get out of these garments. How silly can you be?'

'I can arrange for you to go to the haj in Mecca. It won't cost much.'

She changed into her kaftan. 'I made us some lamb cooked in yogurt.'

Hours later, when she was watering the flowerpots, she looked at the sky. 'If it doesn't cost that much . . . ?'

My mother's job was not well paid, yet she saved up to buy pieces of furniture – a new suite here, a cupboard there – but she never offered to arrange a haj trip for my grandmother. She prohibited religion and all its manifestations.

'It doesn't.'

My grandmother was bent over the sage, her back crooked, hands shaking and her feet swollen. She rubbed a leaf and sniffed. 'Praise be to Allah! What a lovely smell!' She put her fingers against my nose. The scent brought back my mother, her stomach ache, brewing sage and drinking it all night. My grandmother's head came up to my chest. 'Grandma! You're shorter than me!'

'You've grown, Najwa! May Allah grant you a good man, who'll cherish and protect you!'

The setting sun lit up the garden. The tops of trees, water clay jars, geraniums and my grandmother's face glowed in the dusk. We had spent years confined in this house. And the garden was walled, enclosed and overlooked itself. The furthest she had been was a trip to the hot water springs in the south when she was ten. She kept talking about it as if it were yesterday. 'The taxi driver came to collect us on Friday morning. My mother was still alive and had filled a wooden chest with food, salad and lentil risotto and such like. One of the waterfalls was half freezing cold and half scorching hot. One part of you was burnt and the other turned to ice.'

I got her a plastic chair and put it next to the pots of herbs. She sat down.

'It's time for the delicious Turkish delights.'

'There'll be Turkish pilgrims in Mecca at the haj. Don't you think? Will they offer us lokum with pistachio nuts?'

We laughed.

Amman, December 1986

It is freezing cold and I have been looking for Hani again. Two weeks ago he disappeared without a trace. I went to see his parents. After we exchanged niceties and had a cup of tea, they told me that they last saw him fifteen days ago. He came at three a.m. wearing a tracksuit and trainers, packed a bag, kissed his mother's head as she was doing the Morning Prayer and left. He didn't even wait for her to finish worshipping Allah. 'My son, we've not heard from him since.'

It is not like the rascal to disappear without a trace. He would have left me a message at the grocer or the barber. Perhaps the American woman had licked his brains off and he decided to

56

realise his dream and travel to the U.S. with her. But he said that he felt so contaminated after he had slept with her in that cheap hotel that he considered scrubbing his body with bleach. The encounter was 'mechanical rather than romantic'. Perhaps his pragmatism triumphed and he decided to leave. But why didn't he say goodbye?

I searched for him again in all the digs we usually frequent together: the rotisserie, the nut seller, the Old Amman café and the amphitheatre, where we used to sit and discuss past civilisations. I read somewhere that the Greek city states turned into petty kingdoms, then aristocratic oligarchies. The magistrate was elected and then power was concentrated in the hands of the few. The Greeks overthrew the regime and established the first democracy on earth. 'Citizens became rulers,' we would say wistfully as we ate roasted pumpkin seeds. We would spit out the shells and dream about alternative structures of government. Hani said, 'The Greek model was flawed because foreigners and slaves had no rights.'

I gave up looking for him and took the bus to the hospital for the amputation class. I dragged my feet up the hill because, A: amputations, in this country, are rare and most likely I will never use the skill; B: the teacher, whom Hani nicknamed 'Dr Death', enjoys talking about blood and gristle too much and revels in gory details; and C: the sight of severing a limb makes me nauseous.

A body was stretched out on the table in the operating theatre. Dr Death distributed a lecture sheet. 'Amputations resulting from trauma to the limb are usually the result of physical injury, thermal injury or infections such as gangrene. Certain diseases, such as diabetes and mellitus and vascular disease, may also lead to complete or partial amputation of a limb. The development of a tumour may also lead to amputation.'

The corpse, partially covered with a green sheet, must have been of a poor man from the slums of the capital. The unclaimed bodies of dead men are sold to medical staff and students for a few dinars. They organise dissecting parties and cut the limbs to the tunes of Jump For My Love 'You know my heart will make you happy!' When Dr Death began checking his tools – scissors, scalpel, forceps, knife and saw – I held on to my chair. When he began sawing the foot with a weird smile on his face, I had an acid reflux and began coughing. The xur-xur of the saw cutting the tibia and fibula reverberated in the austere room. When he had finished, he held the foot, put it on the table and wiped his glasses.

After watching three amputations, I could not sit in a stuffy bus next to noisy people and listen to the squeal of a pop singer, so I decided to take the number eleven: my feet. It was windy and the dust rose and subsided over the bleak hills. It took me an hour and a half to cross the motorway separating west from east. I walked under pine trees, by villas with green lawns, the royal palaces, an empty valley with a lone goat tied to a peg, and a few houses with corrugated tin roofs. When I arrived at our neighbourhood, I couldn't face looking for Hani again so I went straight home.

Najwa has a toothache: her gums are swollen, her cheeks flushed and she doesn't stop crying. She chews her finger frenziedly. My

58

wife, the organiser of our lives, cannot control her daughter so she looks frazzled and her normally smooth hair is frizzy. I peeled a cool cucumber and gave it to my daughter. She gnawed it as if her life depended on tearing it apart. I sang about a sparrow that stood on my windowsill and asked me to hide it. It twittered its longing for love and safety. Tweet, tweet. Najwa, exhausted, finally went to sleep on my shoulder. I put her to bed.

My wife was crying in the kitchen. She is doing a course on teaching children with special needs. Having a baby, a household, making sure it runs like a Swiss clock and studying at college is too much for her. She cried into the vegetable soup. I held her, but she resisted my touch. Ignoring her coldness, I wrapped my arms around her. She finally wiped her tears with the kitchen towel. 'I added aubergine to the soup today. God knows how it will taste!' My heart understands her need for safety and order, but my head has had enough. We are like an overcooked spaghetti, which was how Dr Death described the nerves coming out of the spine. How can you separate the disc from the cord, the good from the bad? It is impossible; that is why most spinal surgeries fail.

My mother-in-law was squatting outside in the walled garden, inspecting the jasmine. I sat next to her and held her aging hand. 'My son, there is a difference between the quality of air here and in my hometown. It is kinder in Palestine. Your neighbours would cook you chicken with onions and sumac and invite themselves for lunch at your place.' She is missing her village, her late husband and her olive trees.

What is this thing that makes us human? Birth, teething pain, heartbreak, a desire for safety and order? Is it anger, shame, regret or fear? What we desire is unattainable and although we know it, we keep striving for it. Sisyphus, the Greek god, and all that. Xanadu. We used to be situationists and avid followers of Guy Debord. We were the avant-garde, the anti-capitalist, anti-imperialist. 'Secular and holders of the mighty pen,' said Hani. But we were also deluded. How can you stop the advance of capitalism and its degradation of human life and map a different future for yourself? We called our project 'The cosmopolis we wish for and desire'. It was open, secular, civilised: music, lemon chicken stew, women and free love. I kind of understand why my wife is so keen on organising everything, including my underpants.

I calmed the women of the house and went to sleep, dreaming of an eleventh-century cosmopolis where translators of Greek books were paid their weight in gold. Concubines spoke several languages and wore see-through harem pants, even to prayer. They would bend down and you would see their rump, dark and inviting.

A knock on the door at four a.m. woke me up. Hani stood in the darkness, a shadow in white. His mouth was bleeding and his upper incisors were missing.

The Holy Land coach was parked by the roadside. Families gathered around their fathers, mothers or grandparents to say goodbye. A young man stowed suitcases full of clothes, *ihram* drapes and food in the lower hold.

My grandmother stood on the pavement in her long *jilbab* and best headscarf, holding her only handbag: a box made of fake tooled leather. Inside, it had her passport, bus ticket to Mecca and the details of the hotel where she would be staying. I'd carved some money out of my budget and booked her a pilgrimage package with one of the local tour operators. 'The Jewel of Mecca flats. That sounds really grand.' I fiddled with her scarf, checked that she was wearing her watch and adjusted the collar of her cloak as if it were her first day at school. She was teamed up with three other old women going on pilgrimage. The daughter of one of them said that she was going too and that she would take good care of my grandmother, as if she were her own. When they put her small suitcase in the undercarriage compartment she began to snivel.

I clasped her stiff fingers. 'I do hope you have a safe journey to Mecca, Grandmother. May Allah accept your pilgrimage and grant you a place in his paradise!' If my mother heard me she would tear her shrouds.

'Najwa, Allah willing, you'll find your father. I know how much that means to you.' Her eyes filled up.

I could not shed a tear.

She held me, sniffed, then kissed my neck. 'When are you leaving? Don't stay too long alone in that house! Tongues will wag.'

'Two more days.' My right brow arched up.

'May you find your father, *habibti*! May Allah plant good people in your path! May you find love, sweetheart!'

She wiped her face, blew her nose, then was helped up the stairs and into the coach by the veiled young woman, who promised to take care of her.

The sun rose and its light gleamed on the windows of the coach. I could make out the flushed face of my grandmother, her puffy eyes and her trembling fingers. I looked up and waved. She pulled the ends of her mouth upward with her fingers, something she used to do when I was a child. I forced a smile. The driver started the engine. My grandma's hand shook as she raised it and placed it against the glass. I crossed my arms and pressed them on my chest the way my mother did whenever she thought of my father. Light sped on the windows and I could barely see her profile and her beige headscarf. The coach disappeared in the cloud of dust it had unsettled.

The hubbub subsided. I stood for a while. All the clusters of relatives who had come to say goodbye jumped into their cars or waiting taxis and left. The silver leaves of the olive trees, dotting the pavement, shone in the bright light of the morning. There was a chill in the air. It was safe to walk all the way back. I would stick to main roads. Amman was built on seven hills and some blocks of flats, built over years without any planning permission and whenever cash was available, clung to the hills at random. They seemed rickety and tilted this way and that. Standing at the top of one hill, I counted seven mosques. The sight of green minarets, which sprang out here and there, would have appalled my mother. I walked past the bakery, police station, school, the grocer, all the way down to our house.

I unlocked the gate and walked in. The garden felt larger. Mint leaves were scattered on a cloth to dry, a cushion used by my grandmother to rest her feet was by the pot of geraniums and the plastic chair my mother used to use was still under the jasmine. My grandmother kept it at the same angle, although it had been months since my mother had died. She used to sit in that chair and think of you, the man who broke her mind. And on the two stairs leading to the veranda there was a sealed shoebox. The note stuck to the top was signed by Grandmother: *Don't open this until you are about to meet your father.* Her writing was large and squiggly. She claimed that she had forgotten how to write and that she could not read. It must have taken her a long time to write this with her stiff fingers. I put the box under the chair to pack later.

The smell of my mother's cheap perfume clung to everything. I began packing her belongings: suits, cotton underwear, sturdy shoes, socks, tights and a few trinkets. In her wedding photo, she was wearing an organza flower and pearl hair comb. I put it in my pocket. It might jog my father's memory. The nightdress, which she was wearing when she died, was folded, unwashed, in the cupboard. The stink of vomit, sweat and tears wafted to my nose. I turned my head, put it in a plastic bag and threw it in the bin. How did we forget to wash it?

I took the suitcase to our religious neighbour and asked her to give the clothes to the poor. 'The Miss, who gives a sermon every Tuesday, will be happy to distribute them.' Who was this 'Miss'? And how come there were so many women preachers teaching religion all over the place? My mother wouldn't have approved of contributing to the Islamic cause. It was she who drove my father away, not religion. I gave her the suitcase and left.

My clothes were in a pile on the bed. I began examining my shirts, skirts, trousers. The shawl my grandmother had bought from the Pakistani pedlar was already in my rucksack. I tried it on, covered my head with it and looked in the mirror. If it were not for the darker skin, I would pass for my mother. I flung it around my shoulders, wrapping myself in it. The pedlar had told my grandmother in her broken Arabic that women in that part of the world were modest, discreet and beautiful. 'Your granddaughter must hide her flesh! Never look men in the eye: an open invitation to trouble.'

'I always tell her that.'

What would happen if I raised my eyelids? What would they do to me? My skin tingled as I zipped shut the suitcase.

When we first moved in, the sitting room window overlooked a wheat field and now the view was of a block of flats. I emptied the cupboards and gave the shelves a good wipe. I didn't want to come home to a cockroach-infested kitchen. But would I return? An old can full of empty perfume bottles was hidden at the back. Some were small and lilac and others large and green; some had sensible screw tops and others had fancy jar-shaped glass stoppers. Why was my mother collecting them? And why were they hidden? I took one out, opened it and sniffed: the scent of a meadow of iris. I unzipped the suitcase and stuck a few inside – another aide-memoire – between my clothes.

When I went to bed, the house was clean, curtains drawn, the settee suite in the reception room covered with sheets, my mother's and grandmother's beds covered with bedspreads, their cupboards tidy and locked, all electrics either unplugged or switched off and the garden and house plants watered. I planned to slip the key under our religious neighbour's gate before I left. She had promised to take care of the garden and keep an eye on the house.

My flight was at eight-thirty a.m. I asked the school driver, who used to ferry my mother here and there, to come and pick me up at four. I pressed the locket against my palm, rubbed my father's wedding ring, which I wore on my thumb, then ran my fingers over the photograph of his stern face. His dark eyes had a glint in them, perhaps some warmth, but there was a hint of cruelty in the way his lips were set. Who was Omar Rahman? A murderer? A baby-abandoner? A wife-jilter? Or a revolutionary? A chaser of dreams and wider horizons?

At dawn, when the muezzin called for Morning Prayer, I locked the front door, draped some old curtains over the plastic chairs on the veranda and took my suitcase. Dressed in a modest shirt, jeans and trainers, the Indian shawl wrapped around my shoulders, I went out. The school minibus rattled at the end of the alley. Our religious neighbour ran out barefoot, but head covered. My mother had refused to have anything to do with her, although she had lived next door for years. I gave her the key and asked her to take good care of the house. She squinted her eyes, shielded them, then handed me a wrapped parcel. 'This is for you.'

'What is it?'

'A prayer dress made of the finest fabrics.'

'But I don't pray.'

'You might want to one day.'

The driver blew the horn. I put the parcel in my duffel bag and walked away.

'Don't you want to know my name?' she called after me.

I shook my head.

'*Ya Allah!*' The driver revved the engine. Our house began shrinking as we drove off. Men in long white robes and kaffiyehs counted on their prayer beads as they flocked back from the mosque, having finished the Morning Prayer. The seller of hard-boiled eggs and sesame bread pushed his cart up the uneven pavement and parked it next to the shoe-repair kiosk. A man in a shalwar kameez, a so-called Arab Afghani, was handcuffed then led away by two policemen. They looked like giant insects in their hard shell helmets, earpieces, neck protectors and knee pads. Batons and tasers were hooked to their belts. You could not see their eyes behind the visors. The man's friends pleaded with the officers, but they shoved them away, threw him into an armoured vehicle and drove off.

I turned a blind eye. Let them break like clay pots crammed into each other.

Cars, buses, minivans were swerving here and there, trying to park as close as possible to the pavement, where the luggage porters waited eagerly. When we stopped, one of them leapt forward, opened the boot, put my suitcase on a trolley and pushed it away. I thanked the driver and followed him hurriedly before he disappeared into the crowd.

My luggage was scanned then searched. The veiled policewoman patted my body, looking for concealed weapons. It was embarrassing and intimate. My brow was wet with sweat when I went out through the dark curtain. The young porter waved me on. He knew the person behind the counter and my luggage was weighed and checked in quickly. I paid the hefty airport tax and followed the sign to departures.

The policemen in the cubicles had dark tribal features. 'Where to, *inshallah*?'

'Pakistan.' I shifted my weight from one leg to the other.

'Purpose of your visit?' Intense eyes.

'Tourism. I am interested in traditional music.' My grandmother said that they would let me through if I sounded frivolous. Someone who loved to sing, dance and drink alcohol was no threat to anyone.

He stamped my passport and waved me through. 'Have a safe journey!'

Holding my duffel bag, I stood in the middle of the departure hall, disorientated. Where was the border? An air hostess, in a tight skirt and high heels, went up the escalator and I followed her. Our plane was boarding.

There wasn't much in my backpack: my passport, ticket, boarding passes, a toothbrush, a comb, an envelope full of old photographs, the prayer clothes our neighbour had given me, a small radio, a piece of paper with a few hotel names in Peshawar jotted on it, the money in the cloth bag my grandmother had made for me and a letter. 'All that cash! You'd better be careful!' the army officer searching my bag said to my breasts.

I buttoned up my jacket and nodded.

He waved me through.

Through the glass window, the airport looked huge. Aeroplanes were attached to tunnels as if they were feeding off them. Ours was being filled with fuel and loaded with luggage. Everything seemed larger than me and I felt like turning round and running back to the bosom of my grandmother, but she was on her way to Mecca. A line in the sand dividing the world into two had been drawn. On one side lived honourable women, those protected by their fathers or husbands, and on the other loose women like me. I crossed it towards the aeroplane. No going back now. I could see you at the other end, turbaned, bearded and menacing.

Part II

The Bombax Tree

I sat next to a veiled, middle-aged Pakistani woman, who spoke perfect English. She explained to me that the curry we were having on the plane was not 'the genuine article'. She, on the other hand, used chilli powder, turmeric, garlic, paprika, black and red pepper, cumin seeds, bay leaves, coriander, cardamom, cloves, ginger, cinnamon, saffron, mace, nutmeg, poppy seeds, aniseed, almonds, pistachios and yogurt. And I thought my grandmother was into spices. When we stopped to refuel she said that her family's driver would be waiting outside and she'd be happy to give me a lift. My grandmother cautioned me against giving information to strangers. 'Thank you. I'll be met by a friend.'

At the border control, I joined the queue for non-Pakistanis, most of whom seemed either English, American or Indian. The policeman asked the bearded man in front of me something. The answer made him angry. He got up, left his booth, took hold of the man's arm and escorted him away. He returned flushed, eyed me and asked me for my passport. My mouth was dry when I handed it to him. He seemed agitated as he flipped through its pages, then he waved to another officer.

'You don't seem to have a visa.'

'I paid the fee and my passport was stamped,' I stammered.

The second officer came and stood behind him. He flicked through the pages again.

My heart was thrumming.

He looked up then down. He then wiped his forehead and relaxed his jaw. He must have found it.

'Reason for visit?'

'Tourism.'

'Why Pakistan?'

'I am interested in your folk music.'

'Really?'

'"Abeeti" and Sandara.' I swallowed. The Pakistani pedlar, who had ended up stranded permanently in Amman, had told me about old music and used to sing *'Tumhi ho Mehboob mere'*.

He seemed puzzled. He must be wondering why an Arab woman was interested in ethnic Pakistani music. I had to find my father. My grandmother had advised me to look frivolous and flutter my eyelashes. Palms wet over the locket, I said, '*"Tumbi ho Mehboob mere"* and suchlike.'

He smiled and stamped my passport.

I dried my forehead with the end of the scarf, pulled it over my hair and entered Pakistan.

Passengers were greeted by families. They hugged, kissed and chirruped in Urdu, a drawling, dulcet language, similar to that used in Indian films. My mother used to borrow videos from the local shop and watch them with my grandmother again and again in floods of tears. 'Everything is possible in that universe. There is always a reunion.'

'But that doesn't always happen. There is illness, death, cruel hearts.'

My mother mopped her brow. 'Mother! You're such a realist.'

I recognised a few words: '*salaam*', 'love' and 'Allah bless you'. I repeated them in Urdu, '*Salaam, muhabbat* and *Allah barakat.*'

And among the naked and turbaned heads I imagined you standing there with your long curly hair, your fringe tucked behind your ear, your sideburns and full lips, the cruel father who had left me when I was only three years old. I smoothed my long shirt, checked my duffel bag and suitcase, tidied my headscarf and rushed away from the loving chatter of families.

I exchanged five hundred dinars into rupees and left the airport. It was bright but cold outside. I put on my jacket, took my suitcase and joined the queue for a taxi. The smell of spices and perfume filled the air. Rich food was being cooked somewhere not far from here. The sound of Urdu seemed familiar as passengers hugged their relatives, and people greeted each other and exchanged the latest news. When it was my turn, the driver came out, took my suitcase and flung it in the boot. He was clean-shaven, enthusiastic and agile in his long white shirt and blue jeans. I asked him to take me to the Hotel Sadaf.

He hesitated. 'Yes, sure, madam.'

We drove through busy traffic to the city centre. Cars, bicycles, auto-rickshaws, vans and carriages sped by. A bus, with every inch either painted or decorated, stood to pick up passengers. My country's buses seemed drab compared to this burst of colour. Then it raced by with its tassels, fake flowers and hearts, each chamber painted a different colour: bright green, orange, indigo, crimson. The driver was playing bouncy music as he negotiated the traffic. *Allah has willed this* and *A Qur'anic prayer* were written on the bonnet in Urdu – which, to my surprise, I was able to read. How could the driver see the traffic through the densely decorated windscreen? Only the controller, who held on to a bar and flew in the air, seemed sombre in black.

Twenty minutes later we arrived at the hotel, a simple concrete building on a busy road, with a brightly lit grand entrance. I pressed the cloth bag dangling around my neck to make sure that my passport and the cash were still there, paid the driver and got out. A handsome man stood behind the reception counter. I asked for a room on the top floor and checked in. He smiled and handed me my keys, the whiteness of his teeth accentuated by his dusky skin. I thanked him and went up in the lift. When I unlocked the door, walked in and saw the four bare walls, I felt small as if my bones had suddenly shrunk. Our English teacher explained the phrase 'wild goose chase' as a fruitless, futile errand. My mother had died recently, my grandmother was in Mecca doing the pilgrimage, and I was miles and miles away from my home on a wild goose chase, searching for a father I hardly knew. I drank some water, wiped the sweat off my face with a tissue, put essentials in a bag and ran downstairs.

After I visited them, Hani's family sent me a letter. My grandmother found it in the geranium bed one morning. 'They must have flung it over the wall.' It said, among other things, *If you decide to go to Afghanistan to look for your father, you must go via Peshawar in Pakistan. Go straight to the al-Zahrani mosque and ask for Abu-Bakr; he will help you travel through the Khyber Pass.*

'Al-Zahrani mosque, please!'

'That sounds Arabic,' the taxi driver said.

'Al-Zahrani, I am sure.'

'I've never heard of it.'

The first clue was leading nowhere. I panicked.

'Do you mean al-Zaghrani Masjid?'

'Yes, it must be.'

'It's a long drive.'

'That's fine.'

It was an impressive building with triple arches and ornate gates. I took off my shoes, walked on to the cool marble and pulled the veil down to hide my fringe. An old woman with hennaed hair ushered me to the women's section. I went to the toilet, washed my private parts in cold water, went out, then stood by the row of taps. Hands under the running water, I pretended that I was doing my ablutions. I washed my arms, sniffed some water in and out of my nostrils and gargled the way my grandmother used to in secret, afraid to be spotted by her daughter.

'*As-salaam alaikum!*' I said to the attendant.

'Peace be upon you too,' she answered in English, recognising a foreigner.

'What a beautiful mosque!'

'Yes. It is.'

'I love the jasmine outside.'

'Are you a visitor?'

'Yes, a tourist. I am interested in traditional music.'

She wrapped the end of her long emerald scarf around her neck and began to move away.

'I also have relatives here.'

'You do?'

'Yes. I'd be grateful if you could put me in touch with someone.' My voice quivered.

'Allah willing, I'll be able to help you.'

'I am looking for Abu-Bakr.' The whisper was amplified in the spaciousness of the mosque.

She handed me a Qur'an, directed me to a quiet corner away from other worshippers and left.

I sat in the cool space reading it for no obvious reason. In the past I only read it when I was at school and revising for the Islamic Religion course, which I failed year in, year out. A pleasant breeze, laden with the scent of flowers and essential oils, wafted through the arched window. I rested my shoulders against the wall and read.

Have We not expanded thee thy breast? And removed from thee thy burden, which did gall thy back? And raised high the esteem in which thou art held? So, verily, with every difficulty, there is relief. Verily, with every difficulty there is relief. Therefore, when thou art free from thine immediate task, still labour hard, and to thy Lord turn all thy attention.

My mother spent most of her life uptight, drugged and sick. She was angry with my father for leaving us just like that without a second glance. Nothing for her. No letters, photographs or voice messages from him, like the ones received by other families of absent fighters. And that resentment consumed her totally and destroyed her organs. Cancer. If only she had read this verse from the Qur'an, she would have realised that each trial carried the seeds of healing within it. Dry-eyed, I looked through the window. It was the end of winter and there were no flowers on the jasmine.

Pakistan airspace, March 1987

Writing this on the plane. My hands shook. Hani and I were taken to a dark, padded room at the airport and questioned about the purpose of our trip to Pakistan. We told them what we had rehearsed for weeks as we prepared for the journey: 'Export–import. Mangos.' Hani sounded Asian.

'You can get them from Egypt.' He twisted his moustache.

'Not the best, juiciest, sweetest mangos: chaunsa.'

'And now is the season.' Hani felt the gap where his incisor used to be with the tip of his tongue.

'We want to become the Kings of Mango.' I stretched my arms in the style of an Indian temple dance and laughed, an unhinged squeal, perfected for his benefit. The imam had said, 'You must look like two buffoons or else they will not allow you out of the country or worse they might put you in prison for "further questioning".'

He gave us back our passports. 'Don't forget me when you get back with boxes full of delicious mangos.'

'We won't.'

I pinched Hani's arm because it sounded like a threat.

It started that ill-starred night when Hani, a shadow of his former self, knocked on the door. What he had been through forced us to look at ourselves and our country and re-examine everything. He gave me Abdallah Azzam's book, Join the Caravan, and I read it in one go. His words – 'Jihad and the rifle alone: no negotiations, no conferences, and no dialogue' – were repeated in the marketplace, in mosques and houses. He argues that aggressors must be fought wherever they are and that we must rally in defence of Muslim victims, whoever they are. 'We must free Muslim lands from foreign domination, uphold the Muslim faith and create a pioneering vanguard that will form the base for our future.'

'We'll start by kicking the Soviets out of Afghanistan.' Hani held an imaginary rifle.

I don't know why I went along with such drivel. After the ordeal he had gone through, I had this unexplained compulsion to protect him. How many times did I put my love for him and for my family on a scale? How I agonised over this turn of events! But why do we do the things we do? In one of the nursing classes, someone spoke about the power of the unconscious mind, where all your forbidden thoughts, desires and traumatic experiences are stored. Imagine holding a lemon close to your mouth, and it waters instantly. It's like a cruise liner inside your head and no matter how you steer it, it just keeps going in whichever direction it chose for itself. Events are sometimes larger than you.

I began packing in secret, smuggling my clothes, one shirt at a time. I gave them to the barber and he stuck them in a duffel bag at the back of his shop. My wife, busy with her teaching and applications for promotion, failed to notice that my belongings – passport, T-shirts, underwear, books, notes, the Qur'an that my father had given me before he died, which had sentimental value but I never read – were gradually disappearing. When my father said that I would find answers to all my problems in this scripture, I almost burst into laughter. Personal problems: an uptight, frigid wife; economic problems: prospect of no job after graduation; political problems: the sultan ruling supreme. He must be joking. I held up the Qur'an, wrapped in colourful paper, so he could see

81

that I had accepted his gift, but he interpreted my gesture as a desire to uphold the message of Islam and died smiling.

Farewell is fear, a sunken feeling in the pit of your stomach, a checked tear, bitter taste in your mouth, admitting the impossibility of what could have been, acknowledging your impotence and powerlessness and accepting fate. You suddenly let go of the self you knew, the one you had conversations with for years, and welcome a stranger, someone you have never seen before, into your house. Will you and this alien get along as you go on your journey, exploring new maps, searching for new possibilities? And that older self – was it better than this unfamiliar companion?

My mother-in-law was asleep when I kissed her head. She woke up. 'Are you all right?

'I'm fine.'

'You look pale. You're not ill or something?'

'No.'

'You've been staying out too late. I know my daughter is impossible, but she loves you with everything she's got.'

'I know, Nana, I just wanted to make sure you're all right.'

'I am fine, son.'

I kissed her again. 'Go back to sleep, most beautiful mother-in-law in the world!'

She sucked her tooth, turned in bed and looked at the barred window.

My wife was asleep, her eyes rolled behind her shut lids; her teeth ground as she tossed and turned. Although she has no real demons, she fights them all the time, whether asleep or awake. I stroked her hair, caressed her lips, rubbed her back to help her relax. Unwinding her was beyond me. Am I running away from her control and perfectionism? Is that enough of an excuse? Will I regret this? I kissed her lips for the last time.

Najwa, my heart, was asleep in her bed. Angel was written in silver letters on her pink pyjamas. Recently she has begun counting to ten. I overheard a 'conversation' between her and the cloth doll her grandmother had made for her. 'So what do you want to become when you grow up? A nurse, like your dad. Why? They'll give you a beautiful dress to wear, with a tiara and everything. Why? Because you're a princess. Why?'

How do you say goodbye to your daughter? In the same way the Bedouins dry yogurt to preserve it, I tried to store Najwa's features in blue jars, there in the recesses behind my eyes. Her soft olive skin, dark hair, perfect brows, almond-shaped eyes, crooked nose and generous lips. Her hands are like a newly-burst vine leaf, tender, and her fingers are identical to mine: long with oval-shaped nails. I am the one who loves first, sees least and regrets most.

I picked her up, ran my fingers through her hair and checked her cranium, fingers, ribs, vertebra, clavicle, tibia and metatarsals. I tried to memorise the patterns of her bones, the shade of her skin, the roundness of her belly. Her lips were ruby red. Did she have a temperature? I stuck a thermometer in her mouth. She sucked at it as if it were her mother's teat. It showed thirty-six degrees. Normal. If Najwa had had a fever, I would have cancelled my trip. I kissed her eyelashes gently, put her back in bed and covered her *with her favourite blanket, a white fleece with Dreamy Smurf flapping his wings in flight.*

Alone in a mosque in Peshawar, I waited for that kind lady to return. An old woman sat leaning on the wall, repeating her prayers, but instead of counting beads she counted the bones of her fingers. 'Praise be to Allah!' she repeated, digging her thumb into her index finger. There were three bones in each finger and two in the thumb. My grandmother's prayer beads, which she showed me once when my mother was out, had thirty-three beads. She said that you were supposed to repeat the ninety-nine names of Allah and that was why prayer beads had thirty-three beads or any multiplication of that.

I was hungry and tired when the attendant returned. She said that she could not pass on my message.

I held her sleeve. 'I am Najwa, daughter of Omar Rahman. I am looking for my father.'

'I am not sure I believe you. I watched you. You didn't even pray.'

I fished the passport out of the cloth bag. 'See for yourself.'

'It's in Arabic!'

Holding my passport, she walked out of the mosque, her emerald veil trailing behind her. My heart sank. What if I don't see her or it again? I was in a foreign city, surrounded by strangers, without any identity papers. Great. If the police arrested me, how would I explain visiting a mosque after claiming that I was interested in music? What would I do if I could not travel forward or back? I was angry. It's because of you I left my country, my grandmother, and travelled here. It's because you are a cruel father without a shred of compassion in your heart. I hate you. Dry-eyed, I looked at the sky and the clouds gathering then dispersing. I tugged at the locket hanging around my neck like a noose, and spat on it.

The old woman reappeared waving my passport in the air. I wiped the locket with the end of my veil and stood up.

'I made a copy of your details. I'll ask a friend to translate the information.'

'Will you help me contact Abu-Bakr?'

Her gold tooth glinted. 'I'll see what I can do.'

I jotted down a note and gave it to her.

'Now go to your hotel and have some food.'

I put my passport back in the bag.

'Where are you staying?

'The Sadaf Hotel.'

It was getting dark when I left the mosque and the muezzin was calling for Sunset Prayer. The sky was bright gold and streaked with flames of orange here and there. I hailed a taxi.

'Salaam!'

'Salaam!'

He eyed me and revved up the engine.

Amman seemed bare compared to Peshawar, where the

gardens were full of blossoming trees. 'How beautiful, those yellow, white and purple flowers!'

His sipped tea from his flask, gargled then drank. 'OK, madam. The yellow flowers are winter jasmine; the white, loquat; the purple must be magnolia.'

'So rich!'

'We love colour.'

'Back home, houses are either grey, the colour of breeze blocks, or white, the colour of local stone, and gardens bleak. It's dry, mind.'

'Some paint their houses green, yellow and white. We follow Mother Nature's instructions.' He laughed.

We drove through a boulevard flanked by rows of villas, each with a differently decorated entrance. The local stone was rose, like Petra, and they had ornate balustrades and pine-green window shutters.

The driver adjusted his mirror and asked me where I came from.

I changed the subject. 'This neighbourhood is so beautiful.'

'This is a rich neighbourhood. For businessmen, drug barons, arms dealers and suchlike.'

'Is there a big difference between rich and poor?'

'Unemployment, government says, is six per cent. We say fifteen per cent. I have a degree in engineering and drive a taxi. No jobs or suchlike. These houses,' he said, pointing through the windscreen, 'when they advertise them for sale, they also say, "With imported furniture".'

'That must cost so much.'

'Yes.' He sipped more tea and drank without gargling.

I looked at the sky. A moon was barely visible behind the thin clouds. Were you looking at that same moon? What would you be thinking? Would you be wondering about me, your daughter? How my spine, which you used to hold between your large hands, had elongated and spread? Or would you be waiting for the next shipment of ammunitions so you could kill more people?

When we arrived at the hotel, it was dark. I felt queasy and sweaty. My face welcomed the cold air when I got out of the taxi. The doorman stood by the entrance; the gold buttons of his jacket seemed garish in the neon lights. I went in and asked for my keys, balancing myself against the counter. The floor began spinning away in ever-decreasing circles. I panicked. The handsome receptionist with dark glistening hair took hold of my arm.

'I feel dizzy.'

'Have you eaten?'

'On the plane.'

'When did you arrive?'

'One o'clock.'

'No wonder. Please, sit down here and I'll get you some lassi.'

I rested my head against the back of the leather sofa and dozed off.

He brought me a glass full of white liquid. 'Please, madam!'

I drank it. It was yogurt mixed with some fruit I did not recognise and was similar to *ayran*, but sweet rather than salty. 'Thank you.'

'Now, madam, this way. The cook has prepared a delicious meal for you.'

I stood up, leant on him and we walked to the breakfast room together. It was full of tables with colourful cloths and see-through covers. They shone in the dim light. Suddenly I was aware of his arm, hairy and warm, against mine. The pedlar had cautioned me against looking men in the eye. 'Always cast down your glance! Men are easily encouraged.' My gaze went against her advice. His irises were the colour of dark honey, which my mother used to buy from a gypsy. I smiled.

He smiled back, sat me down and went to the kitchen. He came back carrying a tray laden with food and placed a plate, some bread and a small bowl of yogurt on the table. 'Lamb and rice mixed with nuts and raisins.'

'Thank you.'

'My name is Zakir,'

'Thank you, Zakir.' I hesitated before saying his name. It felt like an intimacy.

I scooped up some rice and stuffed it into my mouth.

He laughed. 'Madam must be hungry.'

The food was delicious and fragrant. There must have been cardamom in it, which my grandmother added to everything: rice pudding, chicken, coffee and tea.

The night before she left for Mecca, she handed me a mug of steaming milk and honey with crushed cardamom seeds floating on the surface. 'Your father has absconded, granted, but your grandmother loves you.' She adjusted her headscarf.

The hotel dining room was dimly lit and the evening air carried the sound of a famous piece of classical music. I rubbed my father's wedding ring, still on my thumb.

Zakir came back with a fruit salad. The top two buttons of his shirt were undone and his chest hair gleamed under a gold chain necklace. His nails were manicured and clean. I wiped my hands with the napkin.

Zakir sat down and watched me eat.

The oranges were sweet, the pomegranate seeds red, the mangos juicy and the dates ripe. I swallowed. 'I can hear classical music.'

'Yes. The cook is preparing himself to be snatched up by a famous English chef. He only communicates in English and listens to classical music. It's driving me crazy, yar.'

'They should use it to torture prisoners.'

'I would admit to anything after four hours of Bach. "Yes, I am a terrorist and a member of Al-Qaeda."'

We laughed.

'Why are you here, madam?'

'Najwa.'

'Najwa.' He added a *t* to the end and pronounced it 'Nadjwat'.

'I am interested in Pakistani classical music.'

'And I am Sinbad the Sailor.'

I wiped my forehead with the end of my veil.

'You can trust me.'

He showed me a photograph of his parents standing in front of a tree with red flowers. 'They live in Saidgi. They're bakers.'

'A beautiful tree.'

'Bombax. An English tourist told me that it's called Red Silk Cotton tree.'

His parents seemed hard-working, kind. 'Zakir, I am looking for my father.'

'A beautiful girl like you with no father! Gosh almighty!'

'Yes. And he's somewhere in Afghanistan.'

'Much more complicated than I thought.'

'Will you help me?'

Zakir stood up, looked at the ceiling, rubbed his chin and sat down. 'I'll try.'

I spent the next hour drinking tea, munching pistachio, almond and cashew nut biscuits and chatting with Zakir. He grimaced, frowned, smiled and squinted. When I finally excused myself, Zakir looked ruffled.

I smiled. 'Goodnight, Zakir.'

'Goodnight, madam.' He stood up and pressed his arms against his body as if standing at attention.

The scent of his aftershave and the smell of spices, nuts, rosewater and flowers followed me all the way to my room. He had caressed the lip of the glass with his fine fingers before sipping his tea. I imagined them on my nape, spine and the small of my back. Then I admonished the forbidden.

In a hotel room in a foreign country, listening to distant classical music and the chatter of a television somewhere, I yearned for you, the warmth of your hands around my ribcage, to be safe in your shadow. 'Father,' I said to the dusty curtains, as if you were standing behind them.

The next morning I found an envelope on the carpet with a note stuck to it saying, *I do hope it's good news. Zakir.* I opened it. It was in Arabic: '*Mu'iduna fil masjid*: Meet me at the mosque this afternoon. Pack your bags and bring them with you.' Who sent it? Was it Abu-Bakr? I shouldn't have told Zakir about my father. After my indiscretion the evening before, should I go and meet this contact? What if it were a honey trap? I could end up in so much trouble. But what choice did I have?

I had breakfast – semolina with dry fruit and nuts – then went back to my room and studied the maps and leaflets on the table. I dozed off and when I got up I had a shower, put on a long, modest top over my trousers and covered my hair with the long shawl.

Zakir was standing behind the counter. When he finished checking me out he said, 'Good luck, madam.'

'Thank you, Zakir.'

'I enjoyed talking to you yesterday.' He placed his hand over mine.

'Me too. I never speak openly to anyone. It must be this place – how alive and fragrant it is.' I pulled my hand away.

'Your father comes first, doesn't he?'

I was puzzled by that. 'How can you be without a father?'

'How can you, indeed, Nadjwat?'

'Goodbye then.'

'جب تک ہم سے ملاقات.'

It sounded like *jib tk bm ser mulaqat*. It had 'meeting' in it. I was probably an orphan, a daughter without a guardian father, and there were no meetings or arrivals for me. I bit my lip, lowered my veil and rushed out of the hotel, dragging my suitcase behind me, aware of the tic in my right cheek.

An old man in a wool cap, long shalwar kameez shirt, an embroidered coat lined with goatskin, baggy trousers and leather boots sat by the gate of the mosque. He was cleaning his teeth with a Meswak twig. When he saw me, he stood up, pressed his right hand on his chest and said in Arabic, '*As-salam alaikum!*' He was holding the note I had sent with the mosque attendant.

'Peace be upon you too. Are you Abu-Bakr?'

'Yes.'

'I am Omar Rahman's daughter.'

'I don't believe you.' He spat a splinter.

'You must have seen my passport.' The tic in my face was back.

'Listen. In this part of the world, anyone can forge anything. I can get you a Canadian passport in twenty-four hours.'

'I am his daughter. I assure you.'

'What's his favourite dish?'

I shook my head. 'He left us when I was three.'

'And I am Condoleezza Rice.' He sneered.

'Please. I flew all the way from Amman to find him.' My palms were wet.

'I couldn't give a fig how you came here. You could be a spy, for all I know.'

I swallowed. 'OK. He has a crescent-shaped scar at the end of his left eyebrow. My mother was called Raneen and my grandmother is Zainab.' I showed him the photograph, locket and wedding ring. You stood next to Hani, behind a poppy field, smiling, a young girl with shaggy hair in the background. A few green threads woven in the shape of a star and my name in Pashtu. I pushed your wedding ring back around my thumb.

He stopped cleaning his teeth. 'Did you say "Zainab"?'

'Yes; my Palestinian grandmother.'

He hesitated.

'Please, may Allah protect your daughters,' I said, imitating my grandmother.

'They're all dead.'

'I am sorry.' Panicked, my chin quivered.

'I met him in the Lion's Den.'

Suddenly the lead got hot. 'The Lion's Den?'

'Mujahideen Training Camp.'

'When?'

'Almost ten years ago.'

Then it got cold. 'So long ago.'

'Yes.'

'What's he like?'

'Absent-minded medic.'

'Absent-minded?'

'Always thinking, thinking. Not pious enough.'

'What do you mean?'

'Did not pray regularly.' He spat another splinter.

'Did you?'

'Yes. Five times a day, plus night prayer.'

'Why pray, then train to shoot?'

'Because the world is full of *kafirs*, like you, who are killing Muslims wherever they find them.'

'Like me?'

'Yes. The old woman told me. You don't know how to pray.'

'Is that a crime?' I turned into Raneen, my mother. Her revenge was complete.

'It should be.'

I was about to walk away, then I took a deep breath and began counting trees, something my grandmother had taught me to do whenever I was under pressure. Pine, acacia, carob. 'May paradise be your daughters' final abode!' I'd heard our religious neighbour say that to my grandmother.

He looked at the sky, adjusted his hat, put his Meswak twig in his pocket. 'Fine.'

Masada 'Lion's Den' Training Camp, Afghanistan, April 1987

A relative or a friend must vouch for you before you join the training camp. One of Hani's friends, who facilitated our journey, wrote us glorious references: They are righteous men, with strong belief in Allah and regular observance of his edicts. Upright and honourable, they came here to help us get rid of the red evil.

The five-star camp has seven caverns, each a hundred yards long and twenty feet high, that serve as shelters, dormitories, hospitals and arms dumps. It was built by Sheikh Osama's construction company, mainly to house Arab Afghanis, mujahideen of Arab origins. The beds are comfortable and there is plenty of food, cooked by a Saudi chef.

We woke up to the sound of azan, did our ablutions and stood behind the Egyptian imam in a row on rugs spread outside on the ground. Looking at the bleak mountains in the distance, with a cold breeze on our faces, we cleared our throats, greeted each other, and placed our hands on our bellies. I panicked because I couldn't remember the rituals and I realised that I hadn't prayed since my father took me to the mosque during the Eid celebrations. According to the Islamic calendar, it was the middle of winter, and I remember my teeth chattered as I stood next to him, behind the imam. He believed that religion could be transferred from membrane to membrane by osmosis. If you recited the Qur'an throughout the day, chanted, praising prophet Muhammad, and invoked Allah in a loud voice, your children would one day absorb all your beliefs. I knew what he was up to and it annoyed me. Couldn't I make up my own mind?

I felt like an imposter when we cried 'Allahu akbar' in unison in Jordanian, Palestinian, Syrian, Egyptian, Sudanese and Saudi accents. They would figure it out and deport me. Instead, they patted my back, shook my hand and asked me to straighten the row we were standing in. There is something special about carrying out the same rituals together with a large number of men. Under the influence of proximity, you think that you are related and you begin to prematurely trust them. You eat your breakfast talking about your mothers and their style of frying eggs or making rice and that, you believe, turns you into brothers.

After breakfast, we began our training. Those who do not drive were trained to do so, using bulldozers. On the firing range, a ruddy man nicknamed 'The Hyena' began shouting, 'Grip the rifle! Lift it up! Lie down! Get ready! Aim! Fire!' In a prone position, we fired at the targets – cardboard circles with photos of an American G.I. armed to the teeth stuck to them – missing them all. The Hyena was livid. His white face was blotchy when he shouted, 'Ya Allah! What's wrong with you ladies? If the communist infidel Soviets, lurking in their base a few kilometres away, surprise you, what will you do? Offer them coffee and dates? NO! You're going to shoot and NOT miss your targets.'

And that gruelling regime went on, punctuated by the five prayers. We began to welcome the break of standing and prostrating to God. We were also trained to make explosives and use Kalashnikov machine guns – 'Carry and fire, ninety degrees, projection point UP' – mortars, small anti-aircraft guns and Chinese rockets, a futile exercise if you ask me, because there are no rocket launchers for them.

We also went through basic physical training. Most of us are not fit and some of us are overweight. A young recruit kept falling down as he tried to climb and traverse a rope ladder. 'You're useless! You had too much kunafa *with extra sugar syrup?'*

'How do you know about kunafa*?'*

'Never mind! Just work on your grip!'

'There is nothing wrong with my grip!'

We all laughed.

Lunch was kabsa*, spicy chicken with rice and vegetables. The Saudi chef claimed that he ordered the saffron from 'Sindh, Mahran itself.' It was the most aromatic and delicious dish I have ever had. We ate, cracking jokes about each other's performances Hani was finding it hard to eat the chicken without his front teeth. When I tore it into pieces and placed it in front of him, he smiled. 'Thank you, my friend, for coming with me. I don't think I would have made it without you.'*

Since that night, he hasn't been himself. He rarely laughs and he gets tired easily. The carefree young man who sang Olivia Newton-John's songs has disappeared and now he walks hunchbacked, as if all the worries of the world are upon his shoulders. A house full of music, mirth and lit chandeliers, and then they went in and blew every light bulb, leaving it swamped in darkness.

This evening we gathered in one of the halls, arranged like a mini cinema. A brother introduced a video. 'Muslims, wherever they are in the world, are targeted by the kafirs. We must fight the Russian infidels. It's all connected and one and the same jihad holy war.' The video was a compilation of scenes of Muslim women and children being attacked by Western or Soviet soldiers from Chechnya, Palestine, all the way to Iraq. In one of the videos, entitled 'Infidel Dogs Abusing Muslim Women', American soldiers enter a house, looking for weapons, and kick both the men and women with their boots. A G.I. begins shooting. 'I fucking killed them all!' Then you hear the serene voice of an imam: 'Are you going to safeguard the sharaf, the honour of our women? Are you Muslims? We must protect them and establish a caliphate. They are asking for help and we must answer their call.'

It struck me that the video was assembled, montaged and is historically inaccurate, and some of the shots were too dark to decide who was doing what, but most of the recruits stood up and shouted, 'Allahu akbar!' I excused myself and came to bed to write my diary. I dream of a day, say in fifty years' time, when I will read my narrative, connect the dots, position myself within the larger scheme of things. Will I ever comprehend? Until then, I keep scribbling. Futile, perhaps, like trying to civilise a wolf.

Part III

Acid in the Milk

Abu-Bakr — old, bearded, scrawny and wrapped in a shawl — stood hunched against the morning sun. He gave me the permission he had obtained for me to cross to Afghanistan, a letter and a hundred Afghanis. He said it would be safer to travel unescorted by public transport. 'The driver is trustworthy. Whatever happens, don't say a word! Pretend to be extremely pious and refrain from shaking hands or speaking. If you find Sheikh Omar, please give him my warmest regards. I've made sure that you won't go through Jalalabad.'

'If I keep silent, people might get suspicious.'

'Strict Muslims believe that a woman's voice is *awra* and must be kept hidden. You'll be fine.'

'Thank you.'

He placed his aging hand on my shoulder. 'Safe journey, Allah willing!'

Wearing a chador, head wrapped in a hijab made of a light woollen fabric, I sat in the back of a taxi next to a Pakistani soldier, two farmers and an old woman in a burqa. My mother, who went out of her way to secularise me, would vomit blood if she saw me wearing the blue shroud. I was uncomfortable under all that fabric and kept pulling it from under me and adjusting it around my shoulders. It was cold outside and the windows were closed. I couldn't see the eyes of the old woman, but I could smell her delicate perfume, the scent of fresh flowers. She tore a naan apart and began munching.

The driver wore a padded hat with rolled-up edges over his thick, horsey hair. His green eyes shifted from the road to the mirrors, passengers, then to the road again. The car was old and it kept chugging up the steep hill. We drove round and down a winding road. The valley was flanked with high mountains and you could see the odd poplar tree, its branches like uncombed hair, and a few mud houses in the distance. A young girl, head covered in a green shawl, waved to us. Who was the girl biting the end of her veil and smiling at the camera behind you in the photograph? She seemed at ease.

When we arrived at the checkpoint, we stopped. The soldier got out and joined a group of policemen standing by a hut. The driver pointed at me. I thought he wanted me to get out of the car. He shook his head and waved his licence. I gave him my passport and the permission. He got out, holding the documents, *salaam*ed, gave the two policemen a parcel, chatted with them, slapped his thigh, laughed, adjusted his hat, got my papers stamped and came back. I sighed and smiled. He frowned at me. Smiles, like words, must also be forbidden.

We drove behind an army truck full of soldiers in combat

gear carrying rifles. A trail of black smoke followed it and I could smell the exhaust fumes. Most cars in Amman were old and coughed smoke, polluting the air. The stink of burnt fuel filled the car. I pulled the shawl down to cover my hair and held my breath. The old woman stuck her leathery hand out from under the blue burqa and handed me a piece of bread. I took it then ate it gingerly. Since I'd arrived here, I hadn't seen a single woman eat in public. It must be frowned upon. I held the chador up to cover my mouth and chewed on the bread. It was soft, sweet and aromatic. I squeezed the old woman's fingers and nodded my head.

I felt hemmed in as we drove through the valley, up and down the winding road. There was nothing but shrubs, the odd mud hut and army vehicles. Suddenly the aspect widened and I could see the pointed peaks of mountains in the distance, covered with snow. It would melt, no doubt, and run down to fill rivers and streams. How lucky they are! Jordan is dry and my grandmother rebuked my mother for spraying the plants with water all the time. 'You're wasting so much!'

'Who cares?' She quoted a medieval poet, 'If I die of thirst, let there be no rain after me.'

'He was talking about love.'

'Precisely!'

If my grandmother had been with us, she would have asked the driver to stop and she would have picked a few leaves to examine them later. Is this sage or thyme? She also collected seeds in her pockets to plant later. She was probably circling around the Kaaba in Mecca by now, doing the *tawaf*. Would her arthritic knee hold up? Would she finish the haj she had spent years dreaming of performing? And what about my own pilgrimage? Would I find my father?

We drove by a small lake surrounded by dropping hills. 'It's where the Kabul and Kunar rivers meet,' said the driver, addressing me in the mirror. I clapped with wonder. The wind ruffled the surface and its blueness was emphasised by the bare surroundings. Instead of feeling free as I looked at the vast plain, lake and rivers, my chest tightened and my face twitched: a prisoner watching through bars the world outside. My chin quivered, so I opened the window and breathed in the cold air. It tasted of salt. Once I held my mother so close her tears ran down my cheeks all the way to my mouth. They were bitter, briny. Would I ever taste my own tears? Would I ever soar solo? The old woman objected, raising her arm from under the burqa. I wound up the window.

The driver decided to stop in Charikar. Most houses had obviously been bombed, their walls blackened with soot. I could see shreds of their previous domestic lives through the gaping walls: a red settee, a bed, a jacket billowing on a washing line. The shops were humble with meagre stocks of flour and rice. The sound of scooters and cars, their engines old and rattling, filled the air. Some vendors stood under colourful parasols by wheelbarrows, selling nuts, honey and wheat. People exchanged niceties, 'Salaam! Allah ki taraf, kharid, khada ki mahabat.' A woman holding a yellow voucher was pointing at what looked like green lentils.

Then I saw him. Similar to the policemen in Amman, he looked like an upright insect in camouflage. 'U.S. army,' said the driver. The only Americans I came across were the ones I saw on television. Without my mother's knowledge, I used to stay up late to watch repeats of *The Bold and the Beautiful* and *Love Boat*, in which everyone was slim, tanned and happy. Romance was also on the list of forbidden things in our house. 'Men are predators and they're wired to betray you.' She didn't know how to tend my father and drove him away. Blond men kissed the hands of women and seemed courteous and caring.

And, here in Afghanistan, a real American man stood before me. I had never seen anything like him. He was tall, wide-shouldered, with a neck as wide as the waist of the boy trying to sell him vegetables. He seemed out of place among the red peppers, lettuce and potatoes. He wore sunglasses, a jacket in a brown, tan, yellow and green pattern with the American flag sewn on the sleeve. Holding a rifle, he kept fingering his shoulder pocket, speaking to a gadget, taking photographs and checking a small screen. He haggled with the boy, who now held a jar of honey.

The boy, who was probably used to seeing 'insects', was unfazed. I was unnerved by the sight of him and wondered if he would turn round and shoot me. He might have a gadget that counts your pulse and scans the secrets of your heart, the way they X-rayed my mother's stomach and found the lurking tumour. By now he must have received a fax informing him about my lack of interest in folk music. My hand was sweaty when the old woman held it, slipping me a sherbet sweet.

The driver came back carrying bread, yogurt, tomatoes and a newspaper in English, which he gave me. I read, 'At a press conference, the U.S. president said, "After eight years, some of those years in which we did not have either the resources or the strategy to get the job done, it is my intention to finish the job in Afghanistan."' Finish the job? Judging by the decimated buildings, my father had probably been blown into pieces already. If he were up against the Americans, then he must be dead by now. Was he bayoneted or shot? Omar Rahman, so-called father, traitor, wife-abandoner, must be no more. I hoped that your neck had been slashed with a machete, your heart punctured and your eyes gouged out. I should thank them for killing you. It was what you deserved, after all.

The driver was eating his lunch when someone shouted, 'Motorbike! *Lakna! Lakna!*' He swore, spat out the tomato and tried to ignite the engine. Seconds later, the sound of a blast shook the car. '*Allahu akbar!*' the passengers cried in unison, including the woman, whose voice is supposed to be a taboo. The driver swore and tried again. The engine started and we drove off. I could hear screaming, cries of pain, a siren, some shots. A column of smoke rose against the sky. The American soldier sprayed the bazaar with his machine gun. People ducked. The young boy's white crocheted cap was on fire, his wheelbarrow toppled and his red peppers were scattered here and there.

'A remote-controlled motorbike bomb.' The driver pressed hard on the accelerator and the old engine chugged and spat.

I placed my hand over my stomach. Acid reflux. A grunt.

'Hold it in! Can't stop the car!' He adjusted his hat, his eyes darting around.

My stomach retched again. The old woman gave me a sprig of mint. I chewed it.

'*Staa num tsa dhe?*' She adjusted her burqa over her head. I could almost see her eyes through the embroidered boring holes.

'What your name?' The farmer holding a bundle tied with a rope translated.

I was about to tell him. The driver pressed his index finger hard across his lips.

I shook my head and lowered it.

I had a dream about you once. You drove an old Beetle car towards me then you stopped, opened the door and asked me to get in. When I looked at your face, it was just two overgrown lips with no brows, eyes or nose. I woke up screaming and ran to my grandmother. She got up and held me tight. 'Your father was handsome and he had the most

107

beautiful eyes, the colour of honey in its jars.' She couldn't ask me to recite the ninety-nine names of Allah to calm my nerves, afraid of my mother. 'Recite the names of all the flowers, birds and trees I have taught you, and exhale after each one!'

Jasmine, carnations, daisies, irises, tulips, lilies, orchids. Breathe out! Sparrows, pigeons, blackbirds, nightingales. Breathe in! Carob, lemon, orange, pine, cypress, eucalyptus. Air rushed out of my lungs.

'Fill your tummy with air then hold it in!'

When I had relaxed, I told my grandmother, 'Maybe my dad had eyes, but I couldn't see them.'

The acid burnt my throat and I began coughing. The driver stopped the car, waved me out and pointed at a hole in the ground by the roadside. I lifted the chador, stuck the ends of my veil inside the collar of my blouse and bent down. My tummy muscles contracted again then exploded, pushing the contents of my stomach out. Bile, bits of food and coffee grains gushed out. The woman came and handed me a bottle of water. It was old, the plastic dented and scratched. I drank all the same and washed my mouth. Then she gave me a piece of cloth. I wiped my face and nodded my head, gesturing a thank you. Finally, she produced a perfume bottle, held my fingers and rolled the tip on my wrists. Suddenly we were transposed to a meadow full of wild flowers. I gulped some air then pressed my hand on my heart, a gesture that, I hoped, showed gratitude. She held my wrist and we walked back. One of the weather-beaten farmers stood looking at the peaks of the rugged mountains. He muttered something, pointing at the sky, spat, then got into the car.

We passed by small villages, a few light-brown mud huts padded into shape by hand, one or two breeze-block houses and a mosque. Veiled girls and boys in dirty shalwar kameez and embroidered caps kicked a punctured football by a stream of water, where skeletal cows with protruding ribcages drank. Ammani children had more and better toys: kites, bicycles, frisbees, marbles and yo-yos. They played in the alley, screaming with excitement. Whenever a football fell into the flower bed, my mother would stab it with a knife and throw it back.

The boys would chant, 'It's all right. We don't care, for we have another spare.'

'Shut up!' She would press her hands over her ears.

The sun set, marking the end of the first leg of our journey. We drove through a bustling market town, stretching out at the foot of the mountains, its minars black. There were soldiers, cars, scooters and wheelchairs everywhere. You could hear the dulcet haggling in shops and by stalls. I saw shiny packets stacked on the pavement and I blurted out, 'Biscuits!'

The driver was not pleased. 'No!'

'Yes.' I broke the rules twice.

He swore and stopped the car. I jumped out and ran to

the shop. The smell of tea and spices filled the air. While I inspected the sell-by date on a packet of biscuits, a one-legged boy hobbled by me, his hair long and dishevelled. Another boy hit his crutch and he fell. I helped him stand up. His hand was thin and rough in mine, eyes large, lips chapped. I pulled the edges of my mouth up, ignoring the gesticulating driver. He smiled and 'my heart itched and I couldn't scratch it', as my grandmother would say, describing her love for my late grandfather. I wished I could take him with me, but my journey was arduous and dangerous. How silly can you be? I bought two packets: one for him and another for me.

'*Shukriya!*' He hopped away.

The driver was fuming when I got back. I opened the packet and offered him a Marie biscuit.

'No,' he said in English and pressed down on the accelerator.

We stopped in front a small gazebo with a sign over the door in Pashtu and English: *Girls' School*. An American soldier paced up and down outside.

The driver gave me my suitcase. 'You sleep here tonight.'

I adjusted my chador and walked in behind the old woman. She entered, kicked off her shoes, greeted the veiled woman standing at the back in the makeshift kitchen and removed her burqa. The attendant seemed strong, her arms muscular and her jaw set. The old woman had wrinkled skin, but bright, youthful eyes. The floor was covered with rugs,

110

mattresses and cushions, and there were shelves on both sides full of books. The woman sat down.

I went to the kitchen and pointed at a bottle. The school attendant filled a glass. I gulped down the water. They laughed at me.

The attendant brought us some rice, yogurt and bread. We sat around the tray. The Afghani women said, '*Bismillah,*' then ate. I scooped up some rice with my right hand, the way my grandmother did sometimes. Although there was no meat in the rice, it tasted as if it had been cooked in chicken stock. After vomiting out the contents of my stomach, I was famished. They spoke to each other warmly, probably speculating about me. Who was I? What family? Who were my uncles? If only they knew that the only family I had was my grandmother, who was doing the haj, and my father, who was probably hiding in a cave somewhere in the mountains, or even dead.

After we finished they did their ablutions, then stood in a line and prayed. I felt awkward sitting there and kept fiddling with my pendant. Was I a Muslim? Why did I find bowing to Allah so difficult, even humiliating? Watching believers worship their god was so embarrassing I broke out into a sweat. My mother would run her hand over her uncovered hair. 'It's lonely standing outside the circle of believers.'

I went to the kitchen and washed the dishes. There was a jar of instant coffee on the shelf. I dissolved some grains in water, stacked some biscuits in bowls, dusted each layer with sugar and soaked them with coffee. My mother would have added chocolate, butter and pistachio nuts – her addition to my English teacher's Royal Cake recipe – and then would have left it in the freezer to set. I washed three teaspoons and waited for the women to finish.

I gave them the spoons and pointed at the bowls. They wouldn't eat, afraid of some forbidden component such as pork fat. I pointed at the ingredients: a cup of coffee, pot of sugar and biscuits. They agreed, said something in Pashtu, *bissmillah*ed, then ate. They smiled and shook their heads.

'Good?' I asked, ignoring Abu-Bakr's advice.

The old woman joined her thumb and forefinger in a circle, indicating her approval.

When we finished, the attendant brought us some tea. We drank it sitting on the mattresses and listening to the sounds of the night: a distant truck, a cough, walkie-talkies, a conversation in Pashtu: '*Maakhaam mo pa kheyr.*' It had a /p/ sound, which does not exist in Arabic. I overheard a distant song and was able to recognise the following words: *patience, time, right, human* and *love*. You could live well if you had them.

I checked that my passport and the money were still in the cloth bag hanging around my neck, fingered the pendant and my father's wedding ring, then rested my head on the pillow. I placed my hand on my tummy and pressed gently. My muscles, which had contracted so much while vomiting, ached. I stretched my toes, listening to distant barking, a baby crying and the snoring of the old woman. Holding your photograph against my chest, I imagined you kissing my hand, not the other way round.

I dozed off then woke up suddenly. My heart was pounding. I took in my surroundings. Where was I? A reel of the past few months ran through my mind's eye. The boy next door rejecting me because I was the daughter of a missing father, with little honour and decorum; my mother, thin and bald, bent over the toilet, vomiting blood then filling the plastic ewer with water to wash it down; her concrete grave, which seemed too small for her tormented body; my grandmother's hand pressed against the misty window of the Holy Land coach; your curly hair parted almost in the middle, sideburns, intense eyes as you stood tall and cocky next to your friend, Hani; a boy with his cap on fire, crying for help; the red peppers scattered between the feet of the American soldier.

My hands shook as I poured some water and drank. I blinked. No tears. Nothing, except the sound of my blood pulsating through my inner ear as it raced up to the top of my head. It felt hot. I sat down. *Jasmine, vine.* Breathe out! A baby was crying incessantly. Every hour a bright light was torched against the fabric of the gazebo. I gazed at the ceiling, counting animals: cat, tiger, hyena. Would sleep ever come? When dawn broke, I had no energy or will to continue. There was no 'maybe' about it: I would die in this country.

Aybak, Afghanistan, November 1991

When Hani and I arrived here, we knew what we were doing: we were fighting the communist Soviets and trying to get them out of the country. I was not and didn't wish to be a combatant like him, no matter how hard the warlords tried. They preached, recommended fasting, gave me tapes to listen to, then I was singled out and ostracised. The answer was no. Curing people, not decimating them, was my calling and I was determined to stick to that.

The mujahideen forces were united against the Soviets. When the Americans gave them Stinger missiles to shoot down helicopter gunships, they overpowered their opponents and triumphed. The Soviets were driven out in 1988. Although the pro-Soviet government was toppled, some factions would not stop fighting. They couldn't lift their finger off the trigger. When the enemy that united us was no more, we fractured into gangs. In their bid for power, the mujahideen began exterminating each other and the injuries were mounting.

Under heavy bombardment from the Northern Alliance, we set up a makeshift field hospital in a spot sheltered by the mountains. We spread plastic flooring over the sage brushes, mimosa and thorns, put some mattresses down and set up an operating table with some rudimentary surgical equipment and medicines. We crushed nature, spread grief and destruction. I heard an American G.I. call it 'Torch Earth' on an eavesdropping walkie-talkie one of

114

the mujahideen tuned to their channel. 'Torched Planet', more like. Nothing was spared: old men, women, children, cows, dogs, cats, grass, trees.

The elders decided to promote me from nurse to 'doktor' and I literally spend most of my days here soaked in blood. I had thought that Dr Death's lecture on amputations would be a waste of time. How wrong was I? While he was speaking, I'd listened to Olivia Newton-John's 'Xanadu' on a Walkman Hani had bought the week before.

For the past seven years, and in this desolate place where nobody dared to go, I have performed thousands of operations, mostly amputations. The xur-xur of the saw cutting through gristle and bone has become the only rhythm in field hospitals. Armies on both sides of the divide plant mines as if they are seeds or candies. The whole terrain is contaminated with exploded and unexploded devices.

What I have been doing is futile. Tidying up injuries, making them look neat, puts me at the service of this myth-making machine. I've been busy beautifying this war. I should leave wounds, lacerations, penetrating injuries untreated, gaping and bleeding. Perhaps if we don't clean up the injured, people will wake up to the ugliness of this conflict, this uncivil war.

I have performed single, double and triple amputations, but my worst case was performed on a baby this morning. He was covered with dust, grime and dried blood the colour of chocolate, which it should have been, when they brought him in. He cried incessantly. I held him, put him on the makeshift operating table and removed

115

his nappy, which was full of dry excrement. All his limbs had been blown off willy-nilly, the jagged skin hung loose from his thighs. He was left with a right arm. Thank God for that. If he was going to live then he would need it. I had limited supplies of anaesthetic, so I sprayed his truncated limbs with some lignocaine then operated quickly. With the help of Merzad, a young Hazra trainee, I washed, cut and stitched him as quickly as I could. Throughout the procedure he squealed. How do you turn this mess into order?

When I finished, I began to sponge him clean. As I washed his head, he stopped crying and looked at me with his traumatised brown eyes. I took off my glove and put my finger in his mouth. He gripped then sucked it. Suddenly, I collapsed and imploded as if my skeleton had turned into dust. Najwa, my daughter, must be nine by now, a beautiful girl with curly hair and captivating hazel eyes. And, as I had done almost every day since I arrived here, I wondered what the hell I was doing in this country. Why did I follow my heart and travel with Hani? What am I fighting for? What am I running away from? A controlling wife? In this devastation, my reasons seem feeble.

The baby's right arm, the only limb he was left with, had extremely dark patches on it. I tried to wash them off, but they wouldn't shift. I rubbed frenziedly. Nothing. Skin the colour of ink. It was peripheral necrosis. So a quadruple amputation! For a fraction of a second, I contemplated injecting him with bleach. He would die instantly. But Allah, our maker, forbade killing a living creature.

'Merzad!'

He stubbed his cigarette out and came running. I disinfected my surgical saw and performed a forearm amputation. When we had finished, we cleaned him up, wrapped him in a blanket and placed him on the floor. Merzad and I were both drained, parched. Merzad's chin quivered. He was about to burst into tears.

'Go and get me some fritters.'

'Yes, doktor!'

I knew he wouldn't find any in this hellhole, but I wanted to distract him.

I went outside, leaving the hubbub of the hospital behind — people pleading, consoling, grieving in so many different languages. I sat on a rock away from it all and drank the sweet tea with sage, which some of the relatives of the injured offered to me. Banks of dark clouds threatening rain gathered at the top of the distant mountains. Suddenly, I felt that old age had descended upon me. I am thirty-five and have nothing to show for it. Palestine is still occupied and will not be liberated through Kabul, as Sheikh Azzam promised. Two Gulf Wars later and the tyrant is still in power. Afghanistan is falling apart. A drop of acid was squirted in the milk, curdling it. I spat on the wild flowers and thorns, fixed my turban and made a decision to leave. I will go back to my obsessive wife and ordinary life. I crave simple rituals, like hummus with pine nuts for breakfast on Friday, a swim in the Dead Sea and coming out caked in salt, or shelling roasted watermelon seeds, sitting under the jasmine as Najwa crawls about. Even the orders *of the 'Ministry of the Interior', my wife, seem sweeter than this tea on this wretched morning.*

It was a cold morning. The old woman's teeth chattered as she did her ablutions, prayed, then got dressed. I wrapped myself in the chador and covered my hair. When we went outside, I felt as if we were trespassers. There were no women to be seen. The aroma of green tea, flavoured with cardamom, filled the air. The driver was adjusting his hat over his stringy hair. The two farmers, wrapped in woollen shawls, greeted us, put a wooden chest in the boot and sat in the car, waiting. They were anxious to go home, wherever that was.

After a few hours' drive by towns and villages, we ended up on a road flanked by ploughed fields. I dozed off and when I woke up it was almost midday. I drank some water and wet my face. Right in front of us, nestled between the distant mountains, I could see some buildings. We were heading to a town, finally. That meant some tea and naan. My stomach grumbled. The biscuits we shared at breakfast had been digested a long time ago.

Just before we entered the town, a checkpoint blocked the road. Four helmeted soldiers, armed to the teeth, stood by two jeeps. They raised their guns and signalled for us to stop. I hid my father's photo in the cloth bag and slipped it below my breast. The men were asked to get out of the car first. Spreadeagled, their shawls flapping in the wind, they stood waiting. The driver's jaw muscle twitched when the soldier patted his crotch, looking for hidden weapons. They searched the boot, engine, glove compartments, floorboards, tyres and bottom chassis using hand-held bats with torches and mirrors attached.

They put our luggage on the roadside and gathered around the chest, ran some rods over it, kicked it, then asked the farmers to unlock it. They did. It was full of wheat. The soldiers stuck the barrel of their machine guns into the wheat. Gun oil could seep into the wheat and spoil it. One of the farmers adjusted his hat, looked at the sky and placed his forefinger on his face then smoothed the crow's feet at the corner of his eye. Three soldiers kept guard and one thrust his arm into the grains and sifted through them. I imagined his hand appearing again, holding a bomb or a grenade. It would be the end of us. He could not find any weapons. A sigh of relief!

They waved us out, searched my rucksack and asked the driver a few questions, pointing at me. He told them something, then came back. 'Letter and passport *bas!*' I fished them out. The letter, which Abu-Bakr had given me, was forged by the Afghan Service Bureau in Peshawar. '*This beautiful document is a gift from my people to your father.*' It said that I was a postgraduate student at a fictitious Arab university, studying traditional music. They read it carefully, checked my photograph, inspected my face and spoke to each other. I shifted my weight from one foot to the other and tried to suppress the tic in my cheek. They gave me back the documents and I put them in the pocket, zipped it up and went back to the car.

'No,' the soldier said. He then checked under the back seat and slipped his hand deep behind it. Nothing.

It was past lunchtime when we were allowed to get into the car. The driver swore under his breath and started the engine. The old woman and the farmers gesticulated in anger and relief. The old woman's eyes shone with tears.

We arrived at an austere town as the muezzin called for Afternoon Prayer. It was just a main street with cars and buses parked on both sides, a few breeze-block houses, some with hay or fabric-covered roofs, and two multi-storey buildings. A blue truck full of animals and people parked in front of us. The chickens in the boxes clucked.

The farmers walked away, carrying the wooden chest. The old woman was met by a turbaned old man. He took her case. She adjusted her burqa, turned to me and said, '*Da khoday pa amaan*,' and walked away beside him.

I nodded my head.

I was about to get out. 'Not you! Back!' The driver put on his jacket and went to the shops.

The sky was cloudless and the road stretched right into the middle of a valley. The driver bought bread, yogurt and water. He gave me some food. I was grateful for the simple meal, which tasted as good as my grandmother's best dish: stuffed aubergines with pomegranate molasses. He watched the road, munching naan and chillies, his eyes darting between mirrors: rear-view, side left, side right.

He placed a gun on the seat, switched on the engine and drove out of the marketplace. The soldiers had searched the car thoroughly. Where had he got this weapon? It couldn't have been hidden on his person. He must have collected it from one of the grocers. You look at a face, but cannot see what lies beneath. You gaze at the same spot for years and fail to see the whole picture. A clandestine web began to float to the surface here and there. A spider, which had been living in my house for years, suddenly appeared. How come I had never seen his fine web in corners and cervices before?

We followed a narrow country road, winding between poplar trees and cultivated fields. The sun, about to bid farewell to our world, was setting behind the mountains. Wrapped in all that fabric, I could not sit comfortably. When the driver looked in the rear-view mirror, I noticed that the whiteness of his eyes had a tinge of blue, which made the irises look darker and more prominent. His hair was bushy under the tribal hat, his arms muscular and his fingers strong as he deftly turned the steering wheel, navigating around the many bends.

I tensed up. As the light dimmed, it dawned on me that I was in the middle of deserted fields, alone with a strange man in a foreign country, which I'd entered on a forged visa, without any knowledge of the native tongue. Where were the farmers, the women and the children? And what if he stopped the car and had his way with me? If I cried out, would anyone hear me or come to my rescue?

He checked his mirror again and our eyes met. 'OK?'

'Yes.' I swallowed. He must have sensed my fear.

'Your father, Omar Rahman, good man.'

He wouldn't mention my father before raping me. 'I don't know.'

'You don't know. He good man.'

'Last time I saw him, I was three. I can't remember his face.'

'No. Sad, this.'

I lowered my shoulders and rubbed my neck. 'Yes, sad.'

'*Inshallah* you meet.'

'Have you ever met him?'

'No. Heard so many stories about him.'

'What stories?'

'He doktor, saved life.'

'My father is a doctor?'

'Yes. Doctor Rahman. Save friend life.'

'He studied some nursing, that's all.'

'Carry fighters on shoulder to hospital.'

'My dad?'

'Yes.'

Suddenly we veered off the winding road and followed a dirt track towards the foot of the mountain. I could see some trees in the distance. 'Where are we going?' I blurted.

'Soon safe house.'

'Where?'

'Better don't know location.'

'Will my father be there?'

'Inshallah!'

It was dusk when we arrived at a walled compound. It looked like a fortress. Cows were tied to rings in the stone walls and children chased hens in the yard outside the gate. The driver stopped the car. 'Here.'

Would my father rush out, open-armed, to greet me? Or would he be angry with his daughter for breaking all Islamic rules and travelling alone in the company of strange men? What if his heart was made of flint, as my grandmother had said? Would he reject me? Did he want his past to visit his present and perhaps destroy it? I stepped out of the car and covered my head.

Part IV

Xanadu

I entered the gated compound in the middle of nowhere. Within its confines, a small village extended all the way to the foot of the mountains. There were farms, a mosque with a wooden minaret, straw-roofed houses decorated with holes in their mud walls, courtyards and a large breeze-block building at the back. It was teeming with people, children in colourful clothes and animals. The smell of milk and spices filled the air.

The elders stood in a line, their dark turbans wrapped around their ears and chins, framing their tanned, cracked faces. The women, in brightly coloured burqas, stood behind them, chattering and pointing at me. At that moment of great decorum my chador slipped down, revealing my long top, figure-hugging jeans and trainers. I picked it up and wrapped it around my shoulders, adjusted my veil and walked towards the welcoming party. I offered a handshake, but they pressed their hands on their chests, refusing to have any physical contact with a strange woman. I bowed.

'*As-salaam alaikum lur* Sheikh Omar Rahman *saaqhib*,' they repeated.

The women suppressed their laughter and the girls and

boys ran towards me, encircled me and poked my rucksack, which was on the ground.

'*Wa alaikum il salaam*: peace be upon you too.'

They nodded and smiled. 'Welcome,' someone said.

'Thank you very much for your kind reception.' The English that I had studied since I was eleven turned itself into useful words.

They smiled and inspected me. Were they looking for your features in my face, Father? Were you in me? Any resemblance would be nature rather than nurture. I asked the question which I had travelled thousands of miles to voice, 'Where is my father?'

'Sheikh Omar Rahman?' They gesticulated and dismissed it.

One of the old men gave permission for the women to get closer. One in a pink embroidered burqa walked towards me, shook my hand and led me to one of the houses, a rectangular mud-brick building with large arched windows and doors and a roof made from straw and sticks. I took off my trainers and entered her house. Judging by the number of cushions, mattresses, exquisite rugs, the table in the kitchen and the smell of perfume, they were affluent.

She shut the door, took off her burqa then hugged and kissed me. 'Hello,' she said in a heavy accent.

'Hello.'

She was in her forties, with dark braided hair, kholed eyes and bright red cheeks. Her gold and ruby earrings shone in the dusk. 'Welcome, Omar daughter!'

Odd. She didn't use 'sheikh'. She must have known my father well. I sized her up. She had long legs and a narrow waist, but her shoulders were wide and upper arms fat. 'Thank you.'

'What your name?' She folded her burqa.

'My name is Najwa.' I turned towards the door.

'Welcome, Najwat.' Like Zakir in Pakistan, she added a *t* to it.

'What's your name?'

'My name Gulnar. Mean pomegranate flower.'

Fitting. Her cheeks were as red and her lips as beautiful as the arils.

She called me *farzand*, asked me to take off my veil and relax. When I did, she walked towards me, caressed my hair, traced my brows, eyes and mouth with her fingers, then filled up. The glow of the setting sun streaked through the window and lit up her slightly narrow eyes. The hazel irises and dark curled eyelashes glistened with tears.

We had never met before, so why was she crying? I stepped back.

'Welcome,' she parroted and held my hand.

I shuddered. A shadow must have walked over my mother's grave. 'Thank you.' I was tense and I could feel my right eyebrow arch up.

'Please, sit.' Her wedding ring gleamed in the dim light.

A silhouette stood in the doorway, watched us embrace then disappeared.

I sat on the mattress. She went to the kitchen and came back with tea, biscuits, nuts and dried fruit. I ate the nuts, aware of the noise they made as they cracked between my teeth. She sat next to me, watching every move I made. I felt uncomfortable and lowered my gaze.

She sighed and exclaimed, '*Subhan Allah!*'

Why was she absolving Allah from all evil? Why was she praising him? My face was average and wouldn't merit such wonderment.

'Please, more, chicken nugget!' She pushed the tray towards me.

That term of endearment sounded familiar. My mother used it once or twice. I had a sip of the green tea. It was warm and sweet. A cold breeze. The fine hairs on the nape of my neck stood up. Someone lurked outside the window. Was I being watched? I choked on the pistachios. Who was this woman? Why was she acting as if she knew me? Could I trust her? 'Abu-Bakr sent me here. I am looking for my father, Omar Rahman.' My voice was more solemn than I intended.

'Talk tomorrow. Now rest.' She adjusted some pillows behind my back.

I uncurled my spine, stretched my feet, still in the socks I wore yesterday, and rested my head on the pillow. Clothes, tools, utensils and ropes were hooked to rings dangling from the uneven mud ceiling, which was painted bright green. I was tense, my heart pounded, but I was too tired to stay awake. I dozed off.

*

When I woke up, my host, Gulnar, smiled, showing a cracked tooth, her only imperfection. 'Dinner.' She carried a silver ewer, put a bowl on the floor, poured warm water over my hands, rubbed them with soap, washed then dried them with a white towel. She spread a cloth on the floor, unwrapped some freshly baked bread, placed a large platter of curried rice and mutton sprinkled with sliced carrots, green raisins and pine nuts, a bowel of yogurt and a plate of baked kidneys in front of me. The aroma of cooked lamb, cumin, cardamom, cloves and cinnamon rose in the air. '*Bismillah.*' She poked the mutton with a piece of naan and it fell apart. She scooped some up and offered me a morsel. To my astonishment, I ate out of her hand.

After dinner, I excused myself and lay on the mattress. I must have dozed off again because it was dark when I woke up. My bladder was full and the zip of my jeans dug into my lower tummy. I didn't know where the toilet was and was too embarrassed to wake my host up. The main door was shut, so I lifted the latch and went out. The mountain peaks were dark against a starry sky. I wrapped my grandmother's shawl around my neck and walked on. It was quiet, apart from the sound of snoring and the purring of a motor somewhere. I crossed the canal and walked towards the large breeze-block building with a hay-covered roof, which stuck out at the edges like awnings. I slid the corrugated-iron door open and went in.

The large space was lit by kerosene lamps hanging on the walls here and there. The stink was similar to that of the explosion in the marketplace: a mixture of burnt skin, potassium, charcoal and sweet banana. A shooting range with three targets in the shape of Western soldiers sprawled at the back. I was about to run out when a strong hand clasped my shoulder, its warmth seeping through the thin fabric of my shirt. I glanced at the fingers holding me: strong, dark, cracked with protruding knuckles. An old man. My father? My heart leapt out of my chest. I turned round quickly and, to my horror, my hair brushed the face of the man standing behind me. Growing up in a 'house without religion', as our neighbour called it, I was not used to covering my head wherever I went. Unveiled, I stood face to face with my fate. A masked, turbaned man with narrow eyes pointed his rifle at me. I froze.

'Are you my father?' I twisted my hair into a knot and stuck it into the collar of my top.

Eyes the colour of pistachios inspected me.

'You must be Sheikh Omar Rahman's daughter,' he said in perfect English, still standing to attention and ready to shoot.

Not my father. My ribcage collapsed with disappointment, pushing all the air out.

'Are you his daughter?'

I nodded.

'Why aren't you in the women's quarter?'

'L-Looking for a toilet,' I stammered.

'In the middle of the night?'

'It's almost morning.'

He lowered his rifle and narrowed his eyes. 'Don't come here again uninvited!'

I crossed my legs and clenched my muscles to stop the urine from seeping out.

He led me to the back of the hall. 'This is the nearest one.'

It was a squat toilet with a tap, a pitcher full of water and a bar of soap in a plastic dish holder. A clean towel hung on the wall. I was conscious of the armed stranger standing outside the door. It took me a few minutes to relax my muscles and empty my bladder. I tried to aim to stop the urine spattering the floor and my thighs. Could he hear the splash, washing and drying? When I finished, I opened the door gingerly. He stood to attention, with the rifle slung across his back, his mask lowered. His forehead was dark, brows arched, eyes bright, moustache fine and lips plump and violet. 'Lower your gaze! Don't let men see the colour of your irises! It fans the embers in their hearts.' Not only did I look up, but I also caressed his lower lip with my finger. This took him by surprise. He held my wrist and stepped back. Blushing and hot, I gazed at the tips of my white trainers, now scratched and caked with mud.

He released my arm and sighed. 'Let me escort you back to the house.' He marched ahead of me and I followed. A sweet, sickly smell mixed with the scent of sage filled the air. I realised that what I thought was a rifle was a sub-machine gun. I couldn't see much, so I stumbled over a rock and swore. He stopped.

Darkness lifted, layer by layer.

'Where do you come from?'

'Never mind where I come from.' He looked down.

'You sound English to me.'

'British.'

'What's the difference?'

'You need to live in England for years to understand the difference.'

'Don't you have any loyalty to your country?'

'I do and I don't.'

'Whatever happens to me, I will never turn against my country.'

'I wish things were that simple.' He rubbed his unshaven chin and changed the subject. 'Thank you, Allah, for not granting us all our wishes or whims.'

'Not granting us?' The pointed mountain peaks, now dark against the breaking dawn, seemed like spears stabbing the sky.

'Yes.' He fingered his ammunition belt.

The canal water gleamed, a rippling black mirror between two mounds. Someone was brewing green tea and the aroma filled the air.

'We must accept what Allah, the all-knowing, has ordained for us.' He wiped his face and tucked in the end of his turban, masking his face again.

Here I was in a strange country, early in the morning, listening to a holy warrior preach to me about renunciation of desires.

'What do you mean?'

'Truth hurts. Be careful what you wish for.'

'Truth hurts? Try not having a clue where your father is most of your life.'

'And don't ever initiate contact with a man like that again! You might get hurt.'

So the sermon today was about truth and men. I shrugged my shoulders, leapt over the canal and walked away.

He looked at the sky, checked his turban, ammunition belt and sub-machine gun and strode away, his red *patu* blanket trailing behind him like wings.

It was difficult to go back to sleep after that conversation. What did he mean? Was he trying to warn me? Would finding my father harm me? 'Knowledge sets you free or imprisons you forever,' my grandmother had said. I'd rather know. After tossing and turning for a while, I drifted off.

I woke up to the aroma of cardamom-flavoured tea and fresh bread. Gulnar was in the kitchen preparing breakfast: she scooped, arranged plates and stirred the food in the frying pan. The thin shadow, arms stretched and pressed against the doorframe, darted away when I sat up.

When it arrived, breakfast was almost identical to those my grandmother often prepared for us: toasted pitta bread, thick yogurt mixed with dry mint and olive oil, scrambled eggs, thyme with sesame seeds, tomato and honey. How did she know what I normally had for breakfast? I looked at Gulnar's deft hands cutting the bread, pouring the tea, arranging the plastic sheet on the floor and making sure that the plates were perfectly lined up in front of me. Who was she? And what did she want from me?

She poured water over my hands and I washed them and my face. We ate in silence. The sound of munching filled the quiet house. 'Thank you.'

'My duty.' She pulled the veil over her hairline.

'Why?'

'You my guest.' She tore a piece of bread, filled it with yogurt and ate it.

The food was delicious – fresh, prepared with care – but my heart was heavy and I couldn't savour it. Was that shadow, holding the frame of the door as if protecting itself from an earthquake, my father? Was he apprehensive about meeting me, afraid to be swept by regret? Or was he concerned about being rejected by the daughter he had abandoned years and years ago? Perhaps his heart was too weak to deal with his past, so he was keeping it at bay. My hands were trembling and the honey dripped on my chin. Gulnar wiped it with the fragrant towel, which covered her lap.

'You went out last night?'

'Yes, I was looking for a toilet.'

'You met Ashraf?' She stretched her legs and covered her feet with the towel, a polite gesture.

'Yes.'

'He a good, devout Muslim, all the way from Britain.'

I was there to look for my father and she was distracting me with chit-chat. 'Do you know where my father is?'

She ignored my question. 'My neighbours want to meet you. OK?'

'Do you know where my father is?' Pressure was mounting in the tear ducts under my lashes, but my eyes were still dry.

'They good women. Kind to us.' She held my hand. I shivered. My grandmother's hand had been leathery against the misty glass of the bus heading to Mecca.

The women flocked in burqas in all the colours of the rainbow. They flung them off as soon as they stepped in. Happy to have them in her house, Gulnar embraced and welcomed them. The woman was nimble and jovial, her face amiable, manners graceful, kitchen clean and her tea tray ready. Life was a journey for her, not a source of anguish, like it had been for my late mother.

Her neighbours and friends gazed at me, ran their forefingers over my face as if they were scraping butter, touched my hair and shook their heads in wonderment. My grandmother had told me that I looked like my mother – the same almond-shaped eyes, slightly crooked nose – but I had my father's generous lips and curly hair, which was the colour of chestnuts. Why did they sip their tea, inspect me and then nudge each other? Did I look so different from them? Why did they fondle me like a cat?

One of them, with braided hair the colour of ink, spoke some English. 'Welcome.'

'Thank you.' I tucked my hair behind my ear.

'Where do you come from?'

'Amman.' Would she know where it was?

'Arab, then?'

'Yes.'

'Muslim?'

I had never been asked this question before, so I hesitated. What was I? A believer or a non-believer? Did I have faith? Was being secular a sin? Was it imposed on me by my late mother?

'Family?'

'My mother died six months ago. Cancer. My grandmother is doing the haj.'

'Oh, Allah! Lucky grandmother. Congratulation!' She raised her hands towards the divine.

'Yes.' Lucky indeed. Unlike me, my grandmother knew who she was, where she came from and what she believed in.

She held my hand. 'Sorry your *ma daar* dead.' She then called Gulnar, who was busy chatting to an old woman, and began jabbering in Dari. Gulnar excused herself and went to the kitchen. I could hear her snivel and blow her nose. She washed her face, dried it and came back puffy and flushed.

138

'Nuts?' She held the bowl in her trembling hand.

'Thank you.'

Gulnar was a soft-spoken woman, so I was surprised when she looked through the barred window and shouted at the shadow lurking outside, '*Daukhter! Daukhter! Dur hal hadir!*'

A hush. If you dropped a needle, you would have heard it *clink-clink* on the floor.

A thin, tall woman walked in, her orange burqa trailing behind her. When she took it off, I was looking at a carnival mirror – for it was me, but thinner and with slightly narrower eyes. Her skin was dark, hair curly, eyebrows arched, lips generous, her teeth gapped and eyes downcast with embarrassment. Gulnar held her arm tightly. 'Say hello to Najwat!'

A sheepish 'Hello!' She walked tentatively towards me.

I pushed my double away. Blood raced through my veins all the way to my head and cold sweat broke out on my brow. I mopped it. 'Will someone tell me where my father is? Who are you?'

Gulnar paled. 'Me, stepmother. She your sister, Amani.'

Kunduz, Afghanistan, June 1993

Hani is stationed away from the front line, in a 'five-star' camp near Kunduz, on a break H.Q. give to valiant fighters. They have beds, hot water and local food served by 'fair damsels'. It is like paradise minus the silk cushions, *he wrote. He has been nicknamed 'Sinan', or 'Teeth', despite his missing front incisors. Stories about his bravery have spread far and wide. Merzad, my assistant and source of local gossip, said, 'His machine gun slung on his shoulder, he hops through mined fields like a gazelle courting death. He craves martyrdom. Once he jumped from a cliff thirty metres high on to an American soldier: an Abbas Ibn Firnas, who was the first to try aviation, but without wings.' He pointed his finger at his temple. 'Your friend crazy.'*

I am travelling north in a pickup truck to meet Hani and tell him that I have decided to return home. This endless and meaningless war wearies me. We have been stopped on the way by armed men, who belong to as many factions or armies as there are hairs on my head. Since the Soviet invasion, Afghanistan has become the playing field of all the world's intelligence services: Mukhabarat, Mossad, MI6, CIA. They spy on each other, pull strings, plan entrapments, ambush and assassinate their opponents. All scores are settled here in Operation Scorch Earth and Sky.

We have finally entered the gated compound in the middle of nowhere. Within the walls, a small village extends all the way to the foot of the mountains: mud houses with straw roofs, a mosque with a wooden minaret, courtyards and trees – fig, plum and luquat rise towards the sky. Greenery at last! When I saw a child in a colourful topi and vest, kicking a ball, all his limbs intact, I choked.

Hani ran and embraced me. 'Good to see you, my friend.'

The women, in brightly coloured burqas, suppressed their laughter and the girls and boys ran towards me and encircled me.

'You too, "Sinan".'

He laughed. The broken man of ten years ago is no more.

The compound elders, wearing their pakuls and best vests, stood in a row, their faces weather-beaten and their right hands pressed on their chests. They bowed in unison when I walked towards them. 'As-salaam alaikum, doktor,' they repeated.

A young man translated what an elder said. 'We've heard so much about you, Sheikh Omar Rahman. You have saved so many lives. Our gratitude has no bounds.'

They laid down a feast for me in the mosque: kebabs, pilau, kadu – the famous braised pumpkin – and slow-cooked spinach. They must have slaughtered one of their precious goats for this. I had no appetite, but forced myself to eat. They had gone to so much trouble preparing this delicate, aromatic food. Hani sat opposite me, bursting with pride. 'We couldn't have achieved this if we'd stayed at home.'

'Achieved what?'

'This glory.'

'Do you call this devastation glory?'

My nose is used to the stink of war, the sick and injured: gunpowder, mustard gas, disinfectants, vomit, urine, excrement, gangrene. I've rarely been out to breathe in the fresh air, laden with the scent of wild flowers. A woman in a burqa offered me tea. A whiff of sage, jasmine and thyme. I filled my nostrils. Beyond the mild perfume, I could detect her heady natural pheromones. I

141

experienced an instant arousal. To hide my shame, I lowered my hand, knocking the tray and sending the glasses flying in the air. 'For a doktor, your hands are shaky.'

'I am sorry.'

'Gulnar! Do you still have your late husband's clothes?'

She nodded.

'Take the doktor and give him something else to wear! Ask one of the sisters to accompany you!'

When we walked into her house, she pulled the burqa up, revealing one of the most radiant faces I have ever seen: arched brows, two large eyes with the slight slant of a Hazra, high cheekbones and full, fleshy lips. I imagined them caressing parts of my body that hadn't been graced with a human touch for a long time. I sniffed the air and thanked Allah for creating women, such miraculous beings. If only we dedicated our lives to them, rather than wreaking havoc on this earth.

I changed into her husband's shalwar kameez. 'Thank you . . . ?'

'My name is Gulnar, pomegranate. My husband dead.'

In my mind's eye, I imagined holding a pomegranate. I kissed its skin, scored the rind with a pebble then broke it open. The arils glistened. I separated the peel from the pulp and teased out the crimson seeds from the pith. Their flesh burst open on my tongue, releasing their sweet, sour juice. How delicious were these rubies! Heart beating, lips sticky, hands tinted, I offered my wet trousers to Gulnar.

Ten years without women − except for the odd ugly nurse,

142

foreign correspondent or aid worker – had deadened me, turned me into wood, but one look from Gulnar and sap rushed right through me. Young shoots began to sprout out here and there. In the desert of my heart, an oasis – complete with a pond, palm trees laden with sweet dates, sage bushes, flowers and birds – began to grow. I walked into her house a free man and left a prisoner, shackled, my hands tied behind my back with colourful silk ribbons.

Our wedding vows were witnessed by Hani and Merzad.

When she eased her breasts out of the cups of her bra, they perked up, pushing the now erect nipples forward. My tongue craved the sweet taste of raisins. Was I Qays Ibn al-Mulawwah, the poet who roamed the deserts reciting love poetry for Leila? Perhaps I was Umar Ibn Abi Rabi'ah, the medieval poet who made the pilgrimage to Mecca, not to worship Allah, but to seduce virgins. A gazelle grazing on a desert bush. A camel rocking gently and slowly. I looked for the sea in her, migrating birds, fields of wheat swaying in the wind. I searched for a centre, a walled garden with grape vines and jasmine, my country, an afternoon lull regulated by the gurgling of the fountain, for my wife, the way she was or the way she could have been. Gratified, I reclined on her mattress, a crowned king.

I kept waking up hot, heart thumping, forehead wet and teeth grinding. There must be something seriously wrong with me. I pressed my tummy gently. My mother had died of stomach cancer and her genes, embedded in my flesh, were rotten. They could be poisoning my bloodstream with their bad acids. I didn't know which diseases, hidden in your cells, you had passed on to me. Had I inherited your medical skills? What about your knack for letting people down? Not only had you abandoned me, my mother and grandmother when I was three, you'd created an alternative family and life for yourself. With a beautiful wife and daughter, there was no space left in your heart for us. As in Indian films, I dreamt about you standing there on a plateau, among wild followers, calling my name – 'Najwa!' – and the echo extended its syllables until it turned into the sound of wind howling its longing. I imagined you writing letters, asking me for forgiveness, and all the time you were trying to be a good Muslim husband to Gulnar and father to her daughter, Amani, whose name means 'desires and wishes'.

I tensed up whenever I heard the men outside confer then disperse. I thought I heard Ashraf shout orders. The sliver of sky I could see through the barred window was getting brighter. I tossed and turned. The cows mooed, the dogs barked and then finally the cock crowed. The morning after the night before dawned. When my mother died, the muscles in my right shoulder and arm had cramped and I couldn't move. My grandmother had heated olive oil and massaged them, whispering verses from the Qur'an, a force of habit, for the enforcer of secularism had passed away. 'In the name of Allah the healer and restorer of life!' Half an hour later, my fingers had twitched and I bent my arm. 'Thank God! First your mother, then you.' In this foreign country, and among people I hardly knew, the same thing happened. I screamed with pain.

Gulnar, who was already in the kitchen, kneading dough, came running. 'OK?'

'No. My arm's not moving.'

She shouted orders at Amani, who grumbled then went to the kitchen. Gulnar helped me get undressed. Amani, my nemesis, came back with a bowl full of steaming water. Gulnar dipped a towel in it, wrung it out and placed it on my arm. Her massage was hard, probing, a persistent pursuit of ligaments and joints. Amani, who was not the centre of attention and whose mother's hands were rubbing me, twisted her lips in disgust. Motivated by the rivalry, my fingers twitched. 'Oh! Feeling coming back. *Alhamdulillah!*' Gulnar kissed my cheek. I tilted my head away from her lips. Amani rushed out.

'Let me help you have a wash.'

I listened for your voice among that of the men conferring again outside.

She held my fingers and pressed each joint as if counting them. 'Please.'

I was wearing just pants as she guided me to the kitchen, sat me on a wooden stool, poured warm water over my head, worked up a lather with a bar of soap and rubbed it into my hair. The last time my mother had bathed me, I was five. It felt intimate, but I had no energy to resist. When she finished, she pointed at my pants and left the kitchen. I took them off and washed myself thoroughly. It was an uphill struggle, as if I were climbing Kilimanjaro, as my mother used to say. It had all been an arduous trek for her. Gulnar gave me a towel. I dried myself, wrapped my hair and changed into fresh underwear, trousers and top.

When I was clean, anointed with her perfumed oil, dressed and my hair combed, my half-sister, Amani, sat gingerly next to me. I wished she would disappear, just like that. *Puff!* Magic!

She swallowed. 'I've been learning Arabic.'

'Why?' The shadow of the window bars was cast on the carpet.

'To write . . .'

'Why do you want to write in Arabic?'

She slipped her hand into her shalwar and produced a sheet of paper. 'Here.'

It was like the squiggle of a five-year-old.

Hello, my father.

How are you? We miss you. I hope that it's not too cold for you out there. Mum knitted a shawl for you and will send it soon. Perhaps one day you'll be back for me, for us.

Much love, Amani.

Her lower lip trembled, tears gathered, pearl-shaped, on her lashes then ran generously down her face. My hands were cold. I blew on them to warm them up. I had a half-sister, and there she was, in her embroidered blouse and wide pantaloons, sitting like a bundle of grief on the coloured mattress. She seemed so skinny and young. Her slit eyes widened with sadness and she darted an accusatory look at me as she tried to hold me. I could not touch her, so I shoved her. Hugging her would make her real and I didn't want to admit to myself that she existed. She slapped me. I raised my hand, hesitated, then folded it in my lap. She tried to kiss me and I pushed her away.

It suddenly dawned on me what her letter implied. 'Where is my father?' I shouted and ran out of the house without a veil or chador. Gulnar ran after me and tried to stop me. I pushed her away, she fell and I ran towards the training compound. Ashraf, in camouflage, stood by the entrance. Gulnar got up, dusted herself down and rushed after me. He waved her away and let me in. The place stank of explosives, ammunitions and petrol, and a group of recruits was putting away the fire training gear. He said something to them and they hurriedly tied their bundles and left.

'Please, sit down.' Piercing green eyes.

'No.' I stood by a bale of hay, my hair wet and dishevelled, my face smeared with my sister's tears and snot, and my shirt unbuttoned.

'Sit down!' His jaw muscle twitched.

147

I sat down, snivelled and looked up.

'It's time for you to know where your father is.'

'Really? How kind of you!'

He sat down, got a bottle of juice out of his rucksack, opened it and gave it to me. 'You'd better drink this.'

'No.'

'Please, Najwa!' He looked tired, his eyes bloodshot and eyelids puffy; his trainers were caked with mud and his trousers dirty.

I took a sip.

Someone shouted a *salaam* at him. He said something in Urdu or Persian, then twisted his lip and bit the inside of his mouth.

'Where is my father?' My voice quivered.

He swallowed. 'Your father, Sheikh Omar Rahman, joined the resistance in 1986 and travelled to Afghanistan in 1987. He worked as a medic in Mazar, not far from here. Seven years after he'd arrived here, he got married.'

I rubbed my wet hands on my thighs. 'It took him seven years to forget us.'

'He never did. He spoke about you to other mujahideen.'

'How do I know if what you're telling me is true? You betrayed your own country.' I spat out the juice.

'My country betrayed me first.'

'How?'

'It's complicated. And I am trying to save my country.'

'You're lying to me again.'

148

'Why would I lie to you?'

'To protect me from the truth.'

'I wanted to—'

'Have you met him?' I smoothed down my shirt.

'Yes. Once, before he left.'

'What is he like?'

'Tall, spindly, kind.'

I bit my lower lip hard to stop myself from screaming. The tart taste of blood spread on my tongue.

'He saved so many lives during the bombing campaign in Mazar-e-Sharif in 2001. That's why you're treated with such respect.'

'I heard that he had carried his friend, Hani, on his back.'

'Yes. People say that he pushed Hani's intestines back into his belly, flung him on his shoulder and carried him for miles to the nearest hospital. It was too late.'

'So my father was with him when he died.'

'That was difficult for him.'

'Please, Ashraf, I need to see him. Can I see him?' For the first time in my life I begged.

Ashraf mopped the sweat off his forehead with the end of his turban. 'I am afraid you cannot.'

I pulled out his sleeve. 'Where is he?'

'He joined global jihad and travelled west.'

I howled.

Ashraf stepped back, then forward, held my arms and shook me, his eyes blazing.

I tried to free myself.

He gathered up my hair, tilted my head back and kissed me.

Grief-stricken, I didn't feel his skin against mine. I resisted, twisting and turning.

When he saw Gulnar, he released me. She ran towards me and grabbed me. 'Sorry, daughter.'

'You're not my mother!'

Later that evening, Gulnar's aromatic chicken and rice remained untouched on the plastic plate. She fretted about, smoothing pillowcases, opening and closing curtains, putting the washed utensils away in boxes and then taking them out again. She told Amani off; it was obvious from the tone of her voice. Although my double and half-sister, Amani, unlike me, was generous with her tears. She whimpered an explanation in Dari to her mother, standing outside the back door of the kitchen. Again Gulnar asked me to eat. My stomach rumbled, but I could not touch the food.

There was a knock on the door. It was Ashraf. I overheard his conversation with my stepmother: 'How is she?'

'She not eating. I worry about her.'

Amani stood by her mother, adjusting her veil. She seemed so young and thin in the light of the setting sun.

'It's not easy.'

'No.'

He hesitated, then said, 'Tell her I asked after her.'

'I will.'

'You never know, one day she might be reunited with him.'

'How? He dead? He alive?'

'She shouldn't run out like that, without a veil. Men around here are not used to seeing a woman's hair.'

Amani turned her head and darted an accusatory look at me.

I stuck my tongue out.

'She upset.'

'May Allah bring a good end!'

'Amen.'

'*Khuda hafiz!*'

'Goodnight.'

Amani sat next to me, playing with a cloth doll. Wasn't she too old for that? Probably seventeen, she was acting like a four-year-old. Perhaps you had spoilt her so much that she could hang on to her childhood? You must have showered her with your love. The apple of her father's eye could cry freely. Her tears spurt out at the least provocation. I, the abandoned daughter, on the other hand, weathered and dried-up like a prune, would always remain dry-eyed. I spat then wiped away the traces of Ashraf's kiss.

Amani looked me in the eye. '*Asfih*: I am sorry.'

'Don't speak Arabic. You're slaughtering my language.'

'My father taught me.' She tugged at her doll's hair, made of braided wool.

My heart twitched with pain. 'Why don't you take your doll and go away? You're no longer a child.'

Her slit eyes began to fill up. They shone in the light of the lamp. 'I am a woman, like you.'

Gulnar held her head in the kitchen.

'Why do you play with that doll then?'

'Because my father made it for me.'

At that moment, I could have gouged out her eyes and shredded her stupid doll. 'You're lying. Arab men don't sew and stitch.'

Gulnar's silhouette pressed its hand on its chest.

'He was a nurse. He stitched so many wounds.'

I fished out the heart-shaped locket you had sent me and put it on the mattress.

'My mother helped him choose that for you. He said your name means "a secret whisper at dawn". "So beautiful," he said. He wanted a beautiful inscription.'

I clicked it open. 'What about the few emerald-green silk threads, arranged like an eight-pointed star?'

'I don't know. I have a similar locket with my name inscribed on it.'

Gulnar wrung her hands.

The colourful rugs, mattresses and pillowcases paled suddenly and seemed washed out under the dying light. 'Good for you. Will you leave me alone now? I want to go to sleep.'

She offered me her hand. Her skin was smooth, without

blemishes, her fingers thin and long, with oblong nails, identical to mine. I turned away, stretched out on the mattress and closed my eyes.

She must have gone into the kitchen. I could hear her snivels intermixed with her mother's soothing words and the *mmmwwa* of kisses. Amani was lucky. Throughout my childhood and adulthood I had to soothe my mother, watch over her, lure her away from killing herself. My parents were absent: my father was away and my mother was drugged most of the time. Now she was dead and I blame you for that. Sick with envy, I placed my head on the pillow and pretended to go to sleep.

Amani wouldn't stop whining to her mother. She would say something and Gulnar would challenge it. '*Awnah ihsasat ist brai min. Aya aw haqan khuwahir min?*' I understood the words *feelings* and *really*. Was she talking about me? Or was she in love with someone? Was it mutual? I could detect anguish in her voice. She was desperate to be accepted. Like an animal in the wilderness, its leg trapped, she groaned all evening.

My grandmother's voice travelled all the way from Mecca to my ears. She rebuked me: 'I didn't bring you up to be cruel, Najwa. That family has taken good care of you, housed you, fed you. Is this how you repay them? She is your half-sister. God is compassionate and all-forgiving.' Perhaps my heart would thaw in the morning. Before I dozed off, I

153

decided to give her a hug tomorrow and make a dress for her naked doll, finishing the job my father had started.

Darkness. A blast lit up the house, then I went deaf.

Habash, Afghanistan, 2 December 2001

Merzad told me, as we performed another amputation, that Hani had been fighting up in the north. Under heavy bombardment, their position became untenable. The leaders negotiated a ceasefire, so the fighters drove to Mazar-e-Sharif and laid down their arms. Merzad asked his friend, who works for the U.N. as a translator, to come to the hospital, pronto. In a blue helmet and camouflage, standing on the iodine and blood that pooled on the plastic sheet covering the floor of my so-called operating theatre, she said, 'You see, they were under the impression that the Northern Alliance would set them free. Apparently the Americans wanted to question them about terror networks, so they were transferred to Qala-i-Jangi fortress. They were betrayed. A soldier told me that Hani led a rebellion: two prison guards were killed, the ammunition depot was raided, the southern part of the fortress was occupied and an American General, who said, "I came here to kill you," was captured. No mean feat, under the circumstances.'

I paled.

'Doktor, they put up such resistance. So many British and American air strikes, gunships fired from the sky, smart bombs that

were not so smart; thousands of rounds were shot at them. They gave back the American General's body, booby-trapped. That drove them bananas and they intensified the bombardment. They captured most of the fort. Despite that, the cell led by your friend, which masterminded this amazing resistance, refused to surrender. Alliance fighters shot into the basement where they were hiding, threw grenades into it and finally poured oil in and torched it. This still failed to kill all Taliban survivors or force them to surrender. General Dostum arrived on the scene of the battle and tried to persuade the last prisoners, who were still holding out in the basement, to surrender. His entreaties had no effect. The basement was subsequently flooded with frigid irrigation water. The final Taliban fighters surrendered. Six hundred prisoners who had been brought to the fortress emerged from the flooded basement. Five hundred were killed.'

My hand shook so much I stopped working and sat down.

'I am afraid, doktor, your friend "Sinan" was injured,' Merzad said. 'The gunships are like mosquitoes with red, angry eyes. No chance in hell.'

I dropped everything I was doing and jumped into a truck heading north. I might be able to save him. It was cold and all I could see were decimated villages and craters, their bowl-like mouths gaping. Going round and round in my head was the song 'Xanadu'. It was no longer that imagined space, cosmology, that we had dreamt of. Was it the Promised Land, a dome of pleasure, or hell on earth and this desecration?

It was eerie when I arrived. The hill, on top of which the fortress perched like an eagle, was arid and yellow. The wind whistled as I climbed up with my patu trailing behind me. The stench was unbearable in the yard. Bodies were piled up as if they were sacks of flour. In one room, a grief-stricken old woman held a leg and rocked.

I had to find him.

I tied the patu around my face like a mask and, with my bare hands, I searched through limbs, burst eyes, cracked skulls and leaked intestines. What was shocking was that most hands had been tied, presumably behind their backs. And the bodies had been searched. There was no money, ID cards or gold teeth. One disfigured body after another. Probably six hundred of them.

I went down to the basement, my shoes soaked in human fat and blood. And there he was, dangling from the ceiling, with his hands tied behind his back. The slit in his belly was too neat for a bullet, grenade or explosion. So he was killed, then hanged. I cut the rope, pressed his stomach and intestines in, wrapped his body in my patu and flung him over my shoulder.

Our lives had changed that night in Amman, when he knocked on the door, a shadow of his former self. He told me that the study circle in the city centre had been raided by the secret police and that they were all handcuffed and driven away. He was taken to the intelligence headquarters, nicknamed 'the Oh! hotel' because people were able, sometimes, to hear the cries of prisoners late at night. He said that they had taken him for no reason, because he had never broken the law. He didn't realise that the study group was run by a banned Islamic party.

'The interrogation began in the presence of a foreign officer. "So are you going to overthrow the government?" Hands and legs tied up to the ceiling, I shook my head. "That's a yes, then." I shook my head. "This one is a tough nut to crack." At night, two men came in, broke a bottle and stuck it up my anus, tearing the blastopore and intestines. "He is crying like a woman."'

Weeks later, he was released by one of the many amnesties doled out.

We decided to leave – fight the injustice in our countries, starting here. How misguided we were!

The field hospital was three miles away. I walked through arid land, fields, crossed canals, went in and out of villages, the wind whistling in my ears. People offered me food and drink, but I shook my head and soldiered on. I was determined to get him there and stitch him back together. He might still be alive. Maybe I could bring him round somehow. Birds of prey circled above me, calling. Children, women and elders waved to me then recited the funereal Fatiha verse from the Qur'an: 'You alone do we worship and You alone we seek for help. Guide us to the Straight Path. The path of those whom Your blessings are upon, not of those whom You have cursed nor of those who have gone astray.'

I laid Hani on the table, washed his body with iodine and began assessing his injuries: fractured skull, gouged-out eyes, extracted teeth, stab wounds everywhere, slashed stomach, severed penis, broken knees, extracted toenails. I pushed his bowels, stomach, entrails and colon into place and stitched up his belly.

157

Merzad mustered some courage. 'He's dead, doktor.'

I threw the scalpel at him. He ducked.

I pressed my hand on Hani's neck and felt for a pulse. His body was bruised and cold. The expression on his face was strange, especially because he had no eyes: quizzical, accusatory. His lips were stretched in a triumphant smile. He had achieved the martyrdom he had craved for so long. He believed that paradise was his final home and that seven beautiful houris would receive him at the other end.

I have tried to resist becoming a combatant but unfortunately I've located myself in the middle of this war and, like a hyena, it is claiming me. I've been sitting in this garbage dump far too long not to smell. I can no longer pretend that I am innocent of all the brutality taking place around me. Guilty by association! I should have left when I intended to, five years ago. And now, at my age, I am unable to abandon another daughter. Call it cowardice or compassion. I can't do it. Najwa, my sweetheart, will be nineteen by now. What would I do to see her eyes again and stroke her hair? If there were a bitter dose of regret that would kill me instantly, I would inject it into my veins.

My throat was sore, as if feathers were growing inside it. I threw my surgical needle down and ran outside. The hills and the fields were still there. All that grief! All that desecration! Suddenly my eyesight and hearing sharpened. A sensory metamorphosis. I could hear the rip and chew of eagles tearing up a corpse somewhere at the top of the mountains. My teeth grew longer and hair sprouted out of my ears. It was like that film, Wolf, which someone had *smuggled from Pakistan and we watched in the camp in secret. I leapt from one rock to another, sniffing for blood. A werewolf past midnight; I howled.*

It was a shockwave that could separate skin from muscle. I could see through the window that the sky was on fire. There was no sign of Gulnar or Amani. I got up, opened the gate and ran out, looking for them. Through the dust cloud I could make out a pale-faced crowd, choking on grime. I crossed the canal. Half of the village was razed to the ground and there was no sign of the training compound. Rocks, metal fragments and body parts must have been hurled upwards and then fallen down here and there. An old man without a turban, his grey hair and beard covered with soot, shook his walking stick at the sky, repeating something. I tried to read his lips: Drool? Droll? Drone? Drop? The craters in the ground were full of bodies with severed limbs. Was it an earthquake?

A foul smell, similar to that which filled the air after the explosion in the marketplace, wafted to my nose. The stench of burnt hair and flesh, fertilisers and vomit lingered. I blew out, trying to keep the dust out of my lungs. The villagers, stunned, stood, knelt or squatted motionless. The pits were neat and there were no tremors or aftershocks – so it was not a natural disaster. I looked up towards a sky blackened with smoke. Who dug this abyss in the ground? Who would do such a thing?

I ran from one hole to another, looking for them. 'Amani!' I cried and could not hear myself. A woman pointed at the hills. I couldn't see through the smoke, dust and soot. She held my arm and dragged me away. Gulnar sat, bare-headed, on the stone wall that separated the farms, pointing at the sky and talking to herself. Her head jerked rhythmically. My heart sank because I had seen that crazy jerk before. My mother.

'Where is Amani?'

She mumbled something.

'Where is my sister?' I screamed, but all was silent.

Gulnar pointed at the rubble.

I ran to where the breeze-block building used to stand and began scraping at the ground with my bare hands. There were severed fingers, broken pelvises, feet and scalps. My nails broke. Blood dripped through the *patus* that were knotted into stretchers to carry away the injured. I dug out rocks, shrapnel, shreds of plastic and pieces of cloth, but could not find her. In the stillness, I thought I heard Amani shout, 'Feelings!' My fingers were blistered, but I wouldn't stop.

I came across one of the wood panels that held the roof. I tried to shift it this way and that. Nothing. The villagers saw me and came to help. We counted together and all pushed at once, moving it away. Underneath, there was Amani, lying next to Ashraf. They were both dead. 'Ashraf! Amani!' I cried and couldn't hear my voice. His severed arm was around her and blood trickled out of his glazed green eyes. I tucked his fringe behind his ear, wiped his lips with my sleeve. Then

I looked at what was left of my half-sister. Her jaw was broken and head severed, the locket stuck like an arrow into the side of her neck. When I released it, blood spurted out. I held her fingerless hand. Our handshake came six hours too late. When I nestled her head into my arms against my chest, I could feel her warm blood seep through my shirt into me. I trudged towards Gulnar. The sun had risen, but you couldn't see the sky. Sitting on the wall, rocking and arguing with a ghost, she looked unreal in the faint light permeating through columns of dust and smoke. Unhinged, she repeated something I could not hear.

I trembled. 'She's dead.'

She tugged at her hair.

'What?' Had I gone deaf?

She pulled out a strand.

'She's dead!' I shouted.

She beat her chest rhythmically.

'Amani is dead.'

Her hands shook when she received her daughter's severed head. She smoothed her hair, cleaned her face with saliva, kissed her forehead and closed her eyes. Then she gave me the bloodstained locket.

And, just like that, I left the land of the wronged, of victims and hard-done-bys, and entered the country of the guilty. My heart splintered. How could I give her a hug now? I could stitch garments for her doll until eternity, but she wouldn't see them. In that hush after the drone attack and among the destruction and desolation, I willed myself to cry. Nothing. Her sister couldn't shed a tear.

Part V

Jerusalem in England

On the plane to London, I sat next to a man with blue eyes and funny ears. I thought the British had blond hair, but his was dark. He scribbled in a fat notebook with a rubber band attached to its cover. His clothes smelt of washing powder and the scent of his aftershave was fruity.

I took off my veil, folded it up and put it in my duffelbag. My mother would have been proud, but would my father, whoever and wherever he was?

The Englishman ruffled his hair, rubbed his chin, drew tribal hats, then wrote: *pakol, topi, turban, kufi*. His hands were rough, fingers long with chipped nails. When he switched on the ceiling light, the hair on his arm gleamed.

When the meal arrived, he looked up, rubbed his eyes, blinked, registered my presence and smiled.

Mine was a grin to keep the gapped teeth hidden.

He offered me the salad packet. 'Rabbit food.'

'Wrap-it food?' I was advised to be friendly, so I took it.

'No – *rabbit*.' He placed his thumbs behind his ears, flapped his hands and chattered his teeth.

I laughed.

'My name is Andy. Andrew. It means "man".'

'Najwa. It means "a secret conversation or whisper".'

'How do you say it?'

'Na-dj-wa.'

'Na-dja-wa?'

'Almost there! Keep practising!' I smiled.

He rubbed his ear. 'Much more beautiful than "Andrew", don't you think?'

He told me that he came from a small village in the north, called Bedale, full of old people, closet upper-class alkies and weirdos.

I memorised *alkies* and *weirdos* to look them up in the dictionary later.

'I am like a hoover. I eat whatever you put in front of me. But not lettuce! What's the big deal?' He grimaced.

'Hoover?'

He held an imaginary rod in his hand and pointed it at the floor. '*Vroom, vroom.*'

'Vacuum cleaner!'

'Yes.'

'I eat almost everything, but cannot stand fish with tomatoes.'

'Yeah! That sounds gross.'

The list of words to be looked up was getting longer.

He flexed his rough fingers and told me that he'd been to Afghanistan as a volunteer in a charity that builds schools for girls. 'This thumb is sore.'

I wanted to stroke it, ease his pain, but I clenched my fists instead. I was cautioned against getting emotionally or physically involved with anyone. I turned my head and looked through the oval window at the limitless sky. The clouds stretched beneath us like teased cotton wool, which my mother used to stick in her ears before going to sleep. My mission was clear: to find my father.

Andrew put his hands in his lap and went quiet. He then opened his notebook and began sketching again.

An hour later, he rubbed his ear and smiled at me. I fished out one of the pastries Gulnar had made for me and offered it to him. Just like my mother before her, Gulnar was on a cocktail of antidepressants and tranquilsers by the time I left. She'd stand in the kitchen for hours, staring at the dirty dishes in the sink, trying to figure out how to wash them. When I told her that I was leaving, she started getting up at night, going to the kitchen and making the *bichak*, filling them with sweet pumpkins then baking them. The aroma of cinnamon and freshly baked dough woke me up. 'Amani?' she called me.

'Yes,' I said.

Andy smiled and ate it instantly. 'This is really good,' he said with his mouth full.

'My step . . . My mother made them for me.'

'That's lovely, that is.'

'Glad you like it.'

'My mother is famous for her apple pie.'

'What's that?'

'Cooked Granny Smith apples, covered with pastry, then baked.'

'Granny Smith?'

'Light green apples.'

'That sounds delicious.'

'Would you like to come and visit? What's the big deal? Why would you? How silly of me!'

'Maybe.' I twisted my hair and stuck it in the collar of my jacket. When we arrived, I would have to take it off, and my shirt, and stand half naked in front of the immigration officer.

'Here is my phone number.'

His was the second UK phone number in my address book. The first I had been given before I left, together with two SIM cards and four SD cards, now stitched like buttons inside the sewing kit in my suitcase.

When the aeroplane landed in London, I was surprised to see such giant buildings made of steel and glass. Where was the greenery I heard so much about from my English teacher? Blake wrote, 'Till we have built Jerusalem in England's green and pleasant land.'

'It means green and beautiful, but the text also has a hidden political message,' the teacher had said.

I walked through the metal tunnel, following the sign to the exit. Andy waved to me and joined another queue.

When I arrived at the passport control, the queue was long and wound around the barriers. An old man in uniform directed and ushered us to this counter and that. I took off my shirt, exposing my arms and cleavage, held my passport and waited for my turn. My brief was not to blink, rub my nose, bite my nails, clear my throat, sweat, fidget or smooth my trousers. I must stand like a woman without a care in the world and keep smiling for the security cameras screwed to the ceiling. It was easy not to break out in a sweat in such a cold temperature. To keep my hands occupied and stop them from shaking, I zipped and unzipped the rucksack.

By the time I was about to be directed to a counter, my bowels got weaker and I needed a pee badly. Then I remembered you, my traitor father; I imagined finding you and spitting on your very face and the thought suddenly stiffened my spine. The old man pointed at one of the counters. A bespectacled man with grey hair and a moustache greeted me. When I smiled, my rucksack slipped out of my hand and fell on the tiled floor. *Bang*. The zip was open and my toiletries scattered about. He stood up, then sat down. I collected the empty perfume bottles, lipstick and eyeshadow boxes and put them back.

'I am sorry.' I put my passport on the counter with a steady hand. It had taken me a long time to perfect that. Would he be able to tell that my student visa was forged?

'Najwa Omar Rahman.' He asked me to look directly at the lens and took a shot of my irises.

The muscle in my right cheek twitched and my eyebrow arched up. I pressed my right forefinger on a scanner.

'What's the purpose of your visit?' He pushed his glasses up.

My English, which my mother had invested so much in, evaporated. 'Reason for visit, study at the university.'

'Which university?'

'Westgate.' I swallowed.

'Do you have a letter of acceptance?'

'Yes.' I gave him the forged letter. The printers at the compound had spent ages trying to perfect the colours and texture of the embossed logo. They'd run out of purple ink and had to send someone to Kabul to get some more.

He read it slowly.

'So you are going to study music?' He pushed his glasses up again.

I breathed in, counted to seven, then spoke. 'Yes. I love traditional music.'

He checked my visa again and again, ran his finger over it, screened it.

I tilted my head, pushed up my breasts, ran my finger through my hair and said to the security cameras, 'English weather is what I am afraid of.'

'The university is in the north. It's colder there.'

He ran his finger over my visa again, then examined it.

'Bagpipes. I would like to hear that.'

He stamped my passport. 'You need to go to Scotland for that.'

I tucked my fringe behind my ear. 'Scotland: romantic, no?'

He waved me through.

Nauseous, bladder full, I staggered into England. Did I cross the border, which was a red line between two wooden counters? I went down the electric escalator and saw a toilet sign. I ran in, opened the door of the cubicle, lifted the seat and threw up the aeroplane meal. I flushed down Andy's rabbit salad, which swirled then floated to the surface of the water. I choked, spat, wiped my mouth and went out flushed, sweaty and shaky. An old English woman looked at me. 'Are you all right, love?'

'I am fine. Aeroplane food.'

'Yes, it's all processed and full of *E*s.'

I didn't understand, but nodded in agreement. I washed my mouth with soap and water. When I gargled with it, people gaped as if I was drinking piss. We normally wash the inside of our mouths after each meal, so what's the problem? I inspected my face in the mirror: my eyes were watery, the bags under them dark, my right cheek twitched and my mouth felt droopy. I combed my hair, put my shirt and jacket on and went to look for my suitcase.

Luggage rotated on the large belt and the passengers stood waiting. Andy waved to me. 'Let me help you.'

I tried to compose myself. 'Thank you.'

Other passengers' suitcases stood out, with colourful ribbons tied to their handles or bright labels. Mine was supposed to be indistinct, a simple black affair with wheels and zipped pockets. Yet its contents were very special indeed.

I kept my eyes glued to the belt in order not to miss it. If it landed in someone else's hands, there would be trouble.

Andy helped me place my suitcase on a trolley and we walked out, following the green arrow through *Nothing to Declare*.

'Do you have a lift to wherever you're going?' Andy asked.

'No. I'll find a hotel around the train station.'

'Which train station?'

I got my notebook out. 'Paddington.'

He ruffled his hair. 'I can help you with your suitcase. It's on my way. What's the big deal?'

A uniformed man stood by the entrance to the London Underground. So you cannot enter the city, except through a guarded tunnel. This time I would be arrested. I held my breath, counted to seven and recited the names of trees. 'Ticket machines,' he said and ushered us in.

Gulnar had given me all her savings: a hundred and ten pounds. My father sent her money from England with people couriers. I gave Andy ten pounds.

'It's better if I buy you a card so you can travel all day. You should have your dinner in Piccadilly Circus. Worth seeing, I say.'

'Yes,' I said demurely, searching for the security cameras. What I was supposed to do was check in at the Eagle Hotel and wait for Abu Alaa to knock twice on the door.

Andy sat so close to me in the Tube I could feel his warmth against my thigh. I wished I could go with this kind man to

172

his village and forget about it all, yet your spectre was beckoning me. I looked out through the window, but could only see our reflections for we were still rushing through a dark tunnel. Then we raced overground and there was England in all its greenery and glory! The sun lit up trees, meadows, red-brick cottages, small and dainty, with neat gardens. A tapestry embroidered by divine hands! Blake's 'mountains green' and 'pleasant pastures' shone in the afternoon light. I wished my sister could see this. My eyes dried up and my chest tightened.

'Ahem! Bedale is beautiful, with a green in the middle. You should visit us.'

I said what I had been cautioned against saying, '*Inshallah! Allah willing!*'

When we arrived in Paddington, Andy carried my suitcase to the platform. 'Call me!' he pleaded. 'What's the big deal?'

My nostrils were full of his scent, a mixture of aftershave and sweat. 'Perhaps? Thank you.'

He hugged me and it took all my willpower to stop myself from collapsing into his arms. No emotional attachment!

His blue eyes darkened. 'Bye for now.'

'Bye, Andy!'

Alone on the platform, I waved.

I wheeled my suitcase through barriers and went out of the station. Cars, black cabs and red buses started and stopped down the busy street, their engines revving. The noise of the city was like a roaring river gushing down a cliff. Since I was eleven I had dreamt of visiting London and there it was before me with its churches, cafés and shops. My teacher had shown me the postcards she had received over the years from her English friend, Mr Bell: a phone box, the Thames, Tower Bridge, the Houses of Parliament, Ben Nevis, and a group of men in white playing cricket on an immaculate lawn. 'How glorious!' She had run her finger over the writing on the back.

The newspaper seller gave me directions to the Eagle Hotel. It was getting dark and cold. I walked along side streets littered with rubbish: empty cans, billowing plastic bags and chips. Pigeons feasted on it. A man in sunglasses, talking on a mobile phone, followed me. Was I being watched? I buttoned up my shirt, adjusted the straps of my rucksack and dragged the suitcase across the road. He came after me. Who should I call? The number they had given me? Or this Andy? *What's the big deal?* Then the man greeted a friend and went into a shop.

I rushed around the corner. *Eagle Hotel* was written in red lights above its metal and glass door. When I opened it, it clinked and an Indian man appeared. 'What can I do to help you? Charles, at your service!' He had a heavy accent.

I stood on the dirty carpet, smoothing down my shirt and my English. 'Do you have a single room?'

'Let me see. Yes, we do.' He shuffled papers on the counter.

'Good.' Clusters of dust dangled from the ceiling.

'How long are you staying for?' He wetted the pencil with his tongue.

'I don't know. A week?'

'Passport, please.'

He inspected it. 'Oh! Lovely country! King went to Sandhurst.'

I didn't know what this 'Sandhurst' was. 'Yes.'

'Room seven. Lucky number!'

'Thank you.'

'Hope madam enjoys her stay with us.'

My right cheek twitched with exhaustion.

'If you need anything, just give me a shout.'

'Thank you.'

I went through a narrow, unlit corridor and found my room at the very end. I unlocked the door and went in. It was terrible: curtains stiff with grime, stained carpets, filthy blankets, a torn duvet cover and a mouldy bathroom. I tried to open the window to let some fresh air in, but it was painted shut. I breathed in the dust and went to the bathroom. Cockroaches lay on their backs in the corner of the shower basin by the drain. I gathered them up with a tissue and flushed them down the toilet. I brushed my teeth, washed my face and combed my hair. I unzipped the suitcase, got the sewing kit out, hid it on top of the wardrobe and unpacked my essentials. I changed quickly into a pair of jeans and a pullover, put on my jacket and went out.

I'd never seen so much brightness at night. Electric bulbs lit up pavements, doorways, shop windows, double-decker buses and restaurants. My mission was to melt into this city like a grain of sugar in hot tea.

London, August 2004

What shocked me most when I arrived was the absence of the sound of explosions and weeping. After years of working in field hospitals – and just like schools and mosques they are targeted too – my ears filtered out the noise. Boom: another drone, mine or mortar attack. And that incessant wailing of relatives. Here, I can suddenly hear the silence I have been craving. The carriage we were in glided under the city like a boat over calm water. You could only hear the shunting.

Abu-Hafs, the Taliban warlord, sat next to me wearing his facial mask. He'd been hit by a guided missile and lost his lips, nose, portions of his mouth and the front of his tongue. It fused to the bottom of his mouth and he has to wear a trachea tube to breathe. With the help of an aid worker and an Englishman, who worked for Doctors Without Borders, he was given a visa to come to the UK. They knew a reconstructive and maxillofacial surgeon who was experimenting with new techniques for restoring facial muscles, bones and nerves. They applied for a visa for me as his nurse, companion and interpreter. A few strings were pulled, then a permit to enter the UK was stamped in my passport. I said goodbye to my eleven-year-old daughter Amani, and my wife Gulnar, and packed my gear. They stood at the gate, waving. 'Whatever you do, don't turn your head!' I walked off. My second abandonment was easier, for I am a man with a mission now.

We took a taxi to the address the medic had written on a notepad. The driver kept staring at us: dark, bearded, turbaned and uncomfortable in our shalwar kameez. When we arrived at the assessment clinic and walked through the sliding glass doors, my eyes watered. What a reception area! With the amount of money they had spent on decorations, paintings and flowers, we could easily build a school and a hospital in Kunduz. We sat down in the waiting area, munching a type of pastry and sipping tea.

The doctor is young – barely thirty – yet he is one of the world's top specialists. He is exploring stem cell and other techniques for restoring facial cartilages. His eyes are knowledgeable, but innocent and untainted, unlike mine, which have witnessed the horrors of war. He welcomed us and said that he had a donor and would use his skull to fill in the gaps. The warlord grunted his gratitude.

We took the lift to the third floor. Everything was clean, shiny, new. A spaceship! There was no stink of rotting entrails or gangrene. They gave Abu-Hafs a bed and asked him to change. Nurses fussed. After a few tests, they settled him in without his mask.

The enthusiastic doctor with his perfect teeth explained the procedure. 'After urgent airway management, you need contracture, fistula and sinus formation. We intend to use bone chips carried by artery to construct your cheek, followed by adding local flaps to the

177

face. The orbit will be reconstructed by bone graft, lyophilised dura and Silastic implant.'

I could not understand all the medical terms, but Abu-Hafs' mangled sockets filled up with tears.

I eyed him. 'Excuse me, doctor,' I said, 'but I need to go to my hotel. I'll be back tomorrow for the operation.'

I walked into a peaceful London evening. It took a huge effort to phase out the wails of the bereaved, but the sound of bombardment I left behind resurfaced in this immaculate park, where the roses had been gently wound around a trellis. The din inside my head was unbearable: boom, zurr-zurr, roar, crash, snivel-snivel. The pond was calm and the water was like a sheet of glass, but my mind was turbulent. I sat on a bench and watched an old woman scatter seeds for the pigeons. Even the animals are well fed in this country.

The hotel is basic, but clean and close to the hospital. I had my first hot shower in almost nineteen years and changed into Western-style clothes: a pair of jeans, T-shirt and trainers. I have been away for so long. Why did I leave my family? How could I abandon my daughter? What I go through now must be my penance – the balances and checks of the universe. Now even my toes are hairy and soaked in blood.

I have to learn how to negotiate this new environment quickly, conquer it. Trivial things: local, national and international phone codes; how to use mobiles, maps, transportation; and I must learn cultural references. I would feel better if I were able to locate myself

178

in this maze. I went out and bought various maps of London and its commuting systems. Then I went to a small café, manned by two Indians, and had a curry for supper. I unfolded the first map, turned it this way and that, and began to memorise the streets.

After dinner, I went to the park and stood on top of the highest hill. A whole panorama of London spread out in front of me as far as the horizon. Afghanistan is poor and rudimentary compared to this. Lit-up skyscrapers; mud huts with no electricity or running water. Five different types of juice in a corner shop; no juice. Different kinds of vegetables imported from all over the world; perhaps some tomatoes and eggs. Schools with swimming pools; no schools or just a madrasa in the mosque, if the children are lucky. Shops dedicated to just shoes; stealing the shoes of dead soldiers and stuffing them with newspapers to fit you. Hospitals like spaceships; no hospitals or hygiene, and basic surgical tools. Whoever divided this loaf did not have one fair bone in their body.

I went back to the hospital to see how Abu-Hafs was doing. When I arrived, he had three anaesthetists talking to him. They were preparing him for the operation. The young doctor waltzed in and greeted us. 'How are we today?'

I nodded to Abu-Hafs.

He blinked in agreement.

'Doctor, I have a relative in the Midlands I need to visit. I cannot help with this complex surgery. It might take a day.'

'Shame! I arranged for you to watch the procedure.'

No longer a healer, I said, 'My relative is elderly and I haven't seen him for a while.'

'Yes, of course. If you come back tomorrow morning, your friend will be coming round.'

'Thank you.'

I kissed Abu-Hafs's head. He tugged at my hand. 'See you on the other side.'

'Allah willing!'

I changed the SIM in my mobile and called a number. It rang.

'Yes, we're expecting you.'

I could see the birds perched on the pine trees and hear the dogs barking in the park. Not bad for a forty-seven-year-old jackal.

Stages one, two and three of my mission are complete.

My next task was to go to a mobile phone shop. I asked Charles if he knew of any. He said that there was one by the Tube station and that I had to hurry because they would shut in half an hour. He gave me a map and located it for me. I ran through the streets, trying to avoid people, probably students, businessmen, tramps and policemen. When I got there, the African shopkeeper smiled, which was the first time in London. 'What can I do you for?'

I tucked my fringe behind my ear. 'I need a mobile phone.'

'Contract? Pay-as-you-go? Smart phone?'

A contract seemed like a commitment. I didn't know how long I would be staying in England. 'Pay-as-you-go.'

'A sexy number?'

'No. Ordinary number.'

He got a pink phone out of a box, slipped in a SIM card and dialled a few numbers to connect it, his eyes lingering over my breasts.

I paid him the thirty pounds and left the shop. Men in the old country never looked at you openly and were experts in stealing glances.

Just outside the Tube station, among commuters rushing in and out, with the sound of trains shunting their way into the station behind me, I dialled the number I had been given before I came. It rang a few times. No answer. I panicked, steadied myself, went into a café and sat down. The waitress tried to shoo me away. 'Why?'

'You've got to order something.'

I ordered a tea and held on to the table with my sweaty hand.

Alone in London, without any leads, contacts or friends, I sipped the tasteless liquid.

I was gripped by anger with this father who was supposed to protect me, provide for me, make sure that I was warm and well fed, but brought me nothing but grief. His departure had eaten at my mother slowly until she developed cancer and died, puting an extra burden on my grandmother's shoulders so that instead of enjoying her old age, she had to take care of us and the house, and it had deprived me of any chance of happiness. I could have been married to our neighbour's son by now, but his father wouldn't hear of it. Omar Rahman alone was the culprit. I'd left my country looking for him, found his alternative family, the one he cherished, and here I was alone in this big city on a forged visa. The money was also running out.

I took a deep breath to compose myself. Why not buy a return ticket and give up this futile chase after that deserter, that breaker of promises? Go home and try to get married to an immigrant worker! Loose women would settle for less than indigenous men. The garbage collector seemed always clean and kind. I would live in a room on the rooftop of one of the many buildings, surrounded by wailing children. I would feed them crusts of bread and tea. *Les Misérables*, which we had studied in the eighth grade.

A newspaper seller shouted outside, '7/7 London Bus Bombing Survivor Overcomes Fear!'

Overcomes fear? My mother was not lucid for long and spoke very little. One night I sat in the chair next to her bed, watching over her. Her head was bald and blotchy, her nose blocked with dry blood, hands bruised. When the morphine I injected numbed her pain, she relaxed her grip on the quilt, opened her eyes and smiled. The warmth of her bloodshot eyes wrapped my shoulders like a blanket, but my insides were knotted with anger. She drove my father away.

She wet her lips. 'Najwa?'

'Yes, Mama?' I helped her have a sip of water.

'I haven't been a good mother to you.' She had never said that before.

I sat up.

'It's fear, daughter of mine. Losing your father, I began to build barriers to protect myself from getting hurt again. I vowed not to love anyone.' She wiped her mouth with the back of her sleeve. 'I convinced myself that I would lose whoever was dear to me. Just like that! They would either disappear or die. So I stopped myself from getting attached.' She wiped away a tear.

Dawn broke and the light slanting through the window bars formed patterns at the end of her bed over the colourful quilt Grandma had made. I smoothed it and tucked it around her.

'I couldn't lose you. That would have unravelled me. If you tip a jug of water, all its contents gush out. I wanted to meet my responsibilities towards you and Mother. Sanity equalled not caring.'

In the faint light, she looked like a creature from outer space who had just landed on planet Earth and was trying to learn its language.

'Fear took hold of me and you need courage to live. If I had been brave, I would have got angry, shouted, cried, broken something. I would have travelled the world to look for him. I would have found him and told him what I thought of him. Or, Najwa, I would've had the courage to forgive him, move on, marry the neighbourhood doctor. He doted on me.' She clasped my hand. 'Don't be like me, sweetheart!'

Pigeons gathered over a pizza just outside the door of the café. A black woman wearing tights, a bra and many necklaces, with micro plaits cascading down her shoulders, waltzed across the road. All the passengers on the double-decker going around the corner looked at her. The man sitting on the next table said to the young blonde with him, 'I love you, you silly sausage.'

She grabbed his head with both hands and kissed him. Just like that, in public.

Breathless, he said, 'I'll get a job.'

How did the 7/7 survivor overcome her fear? And what was she anxious about? I emptied the contents of my bag on the table: a mobile phone with two numbers on the memory – Andy's and Abu Alaa's – my passport, twenty pounds and some change, five thousand Jordanian dinars, two gold necklaces, my father's wedding ring, my half-sister's letter, a bracelet Gulnar had woven for me, my grandmother's embroidered shawl, which she had given me before she went to the haj, a forged acceptance letter from Westgate University and some photographs. I put everything back and bought a sandwich and a packet of fig biscuits, the nearest things I could find to my normal diet.

A group of veiled women flocked into the café, arm in arm, chatting and laughing. This was supposed to be a secular country! My mother wouldn't have approved. *'The army of Allah has invaded Great Britain!'* I was about to leave, but decided to stay and eavesdrop.

Their English was perfect. A woman with arched brows and dimples wore a leopard veil. 'He's hot in his black kurta.'

The veil of a younger woman had a golden sheen. 'Who's hot?'

'You know who, girl. Don't muck me about.'

'Oh! Him! Good enough to eat. The halal, permissible way, of course.'

'I am glad you've remembered you're a Muslim. Marriage before gobbling up.'

The girl with the dimples smiled. 'You aim high, sister. You fancy the imam.'

'Just imagine, abstention for years then we get married. The floodgates would open.'

They giggled.

A scruffy young man standing outside the café shouted, 'Oi! Scarecrows! Camel heads! Go home!'

The women seemed accustomed to this. Unperturbed by the abuse, they continued chatting.

'I pity him, if he marries you. You would suck the marrow out of his bones.'

They all laughed. The one with the leopard veil put some gloss on her lips then smoothed it with her finger. 'There's a

185

fund-raising meeting at London Central Mosque – you know, the one in Regent's Park. Just come! There will be food. The sisters go every Friday.'

'Can I come?' I blurted.

They looked at me. The eldest smiled. 'Yes, why not? It's open to all Allah's creatures.'

'I'll try.'

'Where do you come from?'

I hesitated.

They shrugged their shoulders, turned away and continued talking to each other loudly.

I left, buttoned up my coat, bought the paper and walked back to the hotel. If I stayed there for a few days, they – whoever they are – might find me. I could look for a job and embed myself, like an indistinct thread, in the fabric of this city . . . I could join Westgate University for real, but the money wouldn't go that far . . . I could ring Andy, go to visit him and ask him for help . . . Or buy a ticket and go back home and take care of my grandmother until she died. She'd pressed her frail hand against the misty coach window. And after that, who knows?

Avoiding eye contact, I walked back to the Eagle Hotel. The receptionist beamed at me, then winked. I went into my room, filled the glass on the bedside table with water and ate – chewed, more like – my sandwich. It was not fresh and the smell of soggy bread, eggs and cress filled the room. I munched a fig biscuit and had a sip of water.

I sat in bed and opened the paper.

Lisa French, 32, was on the top deck of the number 30 London bus blown up in Tavistock Square by suicide terrorist Hasib Hussain, killing 13 people and himself. Lisa had a phobia. 'Until now, buses have looked like coffins on wheels to me – because that was the image I was left with.'

I looked up *phobia* in my pocket dictionary: *A fear, aversion or hatred.* She had overcome her fear and gone on a bus.

I dozed off and was woken by two knocks on the door; it was past midnight. I leapt out of bed and put on my jacket. 'Who is it?'

'It's me: Abu Alaa.'

I tied my hair back, stuffed my underwear, which I had draped over the chair to air, into the suitcase and opened the door.

An Englishman in jeans and trainers stood outside, his raincoat dripping.

'Come in!' I stepped back.

He placed his forefinger on his lips, walked in and closed the door. A cold wind rushed in behind him. I shivered. For the first time in my life, I was alone in a bedroom with a strange man. I invited him to sit on the only chair by the dressing table.

'*As-salaamu alaikum.*'

Classical Arabic! He must have learnt it in a religious school. 'Peace be upon you!'

'Are you Najwa Omar Rahman?'

'Yes.'

'Can you show me your ID?' He wiped his forehead.

'ID?'

'Identification.' He was jittery.

I showed him my passport.

He read my name in Arabic. 'Fine! I am here to collect the SIM and SD cards.'

'Who are you?'

'Abu Alaa.'

'Do you have any proof?' I'd been told that the cards must not fall into the wrong hands.

'Yes.' He fished a letter out of his pocket.

To whom it may concern:

This is our brother, Abu Alaa, who works as a courier with Islamic Deliverance Front. Please facilitate his mission.

Signature: Emir of UK

I was instructed to give the cards to a representative of the Islamic Deliverance Front. I gave him the sewing kit.

He inspected it carefully. 'Fine!'

I sat on the bed.

'Now, listen to me carefully!' His blue eyes blazed.

'Yes.'

He sounded like a recorded message. 'One: don't open a bank account and even if you get a job, insist on getting paid cash. Two: avoid using computers for anything controversial! Social networks and suchlike only. Three: change your phone number once a month. Just buy a new SIM card. Finally, don't talk about this to a soul! You'll endanger your life and that of others.'

'Endanger lives?'

'Yes. You must be careful!'

I wet my lips. 'What about my father?'

'We don't have much information about him. He arrived in London a few years ago, then disappeared.'

'Disappeared?' I parroted.

'Yes.' He got up to leave.

'Please. I came all this way to find him.'

He hesitated. 'Try this!' He jotted down a phone number on the hotel notepaper, then left. Another chill swirled into the room when he opened the door.

I lay in bed shivering. Who was this Abu Alaa? What type of information was on the cards? Were they going to kill people using the messages I had couriered? If I was not supposed to open a bank account, use a computer or keep the same phone number longer than a month, then I had become part of this network, whatever it was. An illegal criminal? And for what? Delivering the data? 'I hate you!' I shouted at the curtains, stiff with grime.

*

When I covered my body with the blanket, my temperature rose suddenly and I broke into a sweat. My teeth chattered. I tossed away the blanket, took my pyjamas off and stretched on the now-wet sheets. My mother used to have similar fits. She called them 'longing attacks'. My body shuddered uncontrollably. The room smelt of dust, mould and an unspecified acrid stink. What did betrayal smell like? A mixture of his aftershave and the sweat of fear, probably. My father was a coward.

My middle was hollow, as if my diaphragm had caved in and there was nothing to support my ribcage, nothing to stop my carcass from collapsing. Soon, the sound of my insides splintering would fill the air. A man shouted abuse at a crying woman outside my window: 'Fuck you! Bitch!' My body responded by triggering a fever that sped through me. My heart thudded. Drenched, I covered my head with the blanket and duvet.

A crack: the sound of a heart, an arm or a rib fracturing. 'You! Bastard!'

Leeds, April 2005

I travelled north to meet one of the shabab, *who would hook me up with a group of young Muslims called the Islamic Deliverance Front (I.D.F.). My job is to turn them from enthusiasts into professional combatants. So I went to the mosque and instantly* asked for permission to give the imama: the leadership of prayer. I listed my credentials: perfect command of Arabic, knowing the Qur'an by heart and a letter of introduction letter, which ended with a threat.

When I called for prayer, they stood in line behind me. We faced the sacred niche in Mecca. 'Allahu akbar.' I read a short verse from the Qur'an, bowed, then prostrated myself and the congregation followed suit, arching their backs, bending their knees and placing their foreheads on the rug. It was so peaceful in the mosque; you could only hear the buzz of the central heating system and smell the incense and myrrh burning: conditions not conducive to radicalisation.

The sermon was printed in a conversion booklet. I was told that I had to stick to the recommended steps. I adjusted my turban and cleared my throat. 'In the name of Allah the compassionate, the merciful, I think I can speak freely this morning. The likelihood of having an early-rising MI5 agent among you is slim. I was asked about our "extreme" views. Why would a religion of peace have "extreme" views? These commands are all written in the Qur'an. If it has such views, then it obviously is not a religion of peace. But peace with whom and on whose terms? Well, what should we do then? Living under a Christian state, we must unite; we must live like a state within a state until we are strong enough to take over.'

Someone shouted, 'Islam takbeer!'

Others answered, 'Allahu akbar!'

I have called my course 'Get Even – Closer to Allah'. You lure them away from their friends and family, prescribe extra praying, continual fasting, then abstinence. The bombers have to be 'cleanskins', totally unknown to the police. Out of the hardcore, who attended every prayer, I have chosen four. They have an innocence and naivety about them that you see only on the faces of those who think they can change the world. I befriended them, invited them to dinners of chicken and rice, cracked jokes with them about girls and sex, even watched films with them. Then I began to question their identities and made them feel guilty about their silence. They were accessories to the murders of fellow Muslims. I have also given them books to read and tapes to listen to. Now, slowly, they – yes, they – are beginning to suggest a way out, a rebirth.

Teaching them how to make a simple explosive was a nightmare. They had neither the inclination nor the dedication. Also, their minds are saturated with dunia: the lights and distractions of the West – iPhone, iWant, iLove, all decadent and instantaneous. You drink pleasure and self-gratification and it leaves you empty and thirsty for more. Just buying the ingredients for the damned bomb was difficult to organise. A simple mixing of ammonium nitrate fertiliser, sulphate, hydrogen peroxide and acetone was beyond them and they almost detonated the bomb while making it. As for wiring themselves up and setting the timer, it has taken them a month to learn. They would miss the session to go to a Green Day concert or a stag do, whatever that is. So I have had to lure them back and go through the manual, which I smuggled in my luggage, once again with the precision of an ex-doktor.

*

We recorded a martyrdom video against the black flag of al-Qaeda. 'I and thousands like me are forsaking everything for what we believe in. Our drive and motivation doesn't come from tangible commodities that this world has to offer, but from our faith, Islam. Your democratically elected governments continuously perpetuate atrocities against my people all over the world. And your support of them makes you directly responsible. Until we feel secure, you will be our targets. Until you stop the bombing, gassing, imprisonment and torture of Muslims, we will not stop this fight. We are at war and I am a soldier. Now you too will have a taste of your own medicine.'

The attacks were supposed to take place today, but the hired van, which the shabab will drive to Luton, did not arrive on time. I ordered them to abort, but it was like reining in hungry dogs. I have watched them tear corpses with their incisors after a drone attack. Those who remained alive shooed them away. It has to go according to plan to cause maximum damage and grief. The bombs have to be detonated during the rush hour. Those are the orders of the emir.

I have come back to the safe house, but I can't sleep a wink. Will what we have planned for years finally happen? And if it does, will it be the piece of art we have designed? You are not as good as your plan, but as good as the combatants on the ground.

I put the TV on and waited. A report said that at eight-fifty a.m. a power surge in the Underground caused explosions in the circuits. Then a few hours later the Home Secretary confirmed that they *were terrorist attacks. Three bombs were detonated on the London Underground trains within fifty seconds of each other. An hour after the attack, another bomb was detonated on board a double-decker bus. The last one was my gift to the emir, who had reminisced about boarding such a bus on one of his visits to London.*

Then the images of the carnage began to be beamed: emergency services blocking the roads; a mangled red bus with the top deck blown off; a medic pressing a white cloth mask to a woman's face; Underground tunnels blown up, their wires and cables dangling all the way to the rails; a shocked, bloodied man emerging from the station, coughing. Then some C.C.T.V. footage of the bombers with their lethal rucksacks on their backs. That was the last recording of them before they sacrificed themselves for Allah.

A mixture of feelings: exhilaration followed by sadness, then fear followed by anger. I am elated that some of the hell they have dropped on us in Afghanistan has been transposed. You cannot turn a blind eye to an atrocity taking place miles and miles away, thinking that it will not be visited upon you. Natural laws of extension. Sad that the young men had to die. Afraid of the random arrests of the innocent and guilty. Muslims will be ostracised, whether they live in so-called Islamic countries or in the kafir *West. Angry because the world, its politics, the mess I find myself in, has conspired against me and brought me so far, all the way from healing to hurting. I have forsaken everything for my beliefs.*

I stayed in bed for three days, having one spasm after another. When gripped by fear, my muscles would convulse, my teeth chatter, heart pound and vision blur. The attack would tingle its way down me like an electric current. Was I dying in this filthy hotel room in the middle of London? My skin was pale and covered with scabs, there were dark bags under my eyes, my tummy was bloated and I burped all the time. It must be stomach cancer. Like mother, like daughter.

Going to the toilet felt like climbing Ben Nevis, the highest mountain in the UK. Mr Bell, my English teacher's friend, sent her a postcard of it when he visited the Scottish Highlands. It had looked menacing under the grey sky. Shaking, I would balance myself and will my feet to shuffle towards the bathroom. I sat on the bowl and pressed my tummy, trying to defecate; then, with the brush, I checked my stool for blood the way my mother did. 'Where is my father, this angel of mercy?' I shouted at the mouldy tiles, then threw the brush in the shower tray. It drew a line of shit against the ceramic. When I looked in the mirror, my reflection was of someone I barely knew. I had a tic on the left side of my face, my neck jerked and my tongue was furry. I drank straight from the tap and went back to bed.

Could you inadvertently betray your half-sister twice? My mother often quoted Shakespeare, 'Though those that are betrayed do feel the treason sharply, yet the traitor stands in worse case of woe.' When she translated the quote to my grandmother, she said that Shakespeare had the passion of an Arab. Why was Ashraf lying right next to Amani? Were they lovers? Why did I caress his lower lip and later allow him to kiss me? Imagining myself holding her head, I re-read my half-sister's letter:

Hello, my father.

How are you? We miss you. I hope that it's not too cold for you out there. Mum knitted a shawl for you and will send it soon. Perhaps one day you'll be back for me, for us.

Much love, Amani.

Back for her? What about me? My stomach cramped and I screamed in agony.

But she had been deserted too and I wouldn't console or hold her. My grandmother advised me to follow my gut feeling. 'It's there between the ribs and under the heart.' It tightened that day and impelled me to hug her, but my compass was clouded by anger and fear. I was livid with my father, who had forgotten all about me. If only I had told her that I cared. Her blood, still warm, seeped through my shirt then trickled down my breasts and belly all the way to my thighs.

I was drenched in sweat when the receptionist knocked on the door. 'Are you OK? Not seen you for a while.'

I didn't answer.

He used his master key, unlocked the door and rushed in, pinching his nose with his thumb and forefinger. 'Oh! My God! What's this smell?'

I turned my head away.

He tried to open the window, pushing it up, and failed. He rushed to the toilet and saw the patterns of shit drawn everywhere. 'Disgusting!'

He shook my shoulder.

I shut my eyes firmly.

He switched on my mobile phone, scrolled down and rang Andy. 'There's a young woman here. Her name is Najwa. She's in a state. You'd better come quickly.' Then he rang the cleaner and asked her to come pronto to clean up 'this mess'.

Andy arrived that afternoon. 'Najwa?'

A familiar voice. I opened my eyes. Standing above me, his ears seemed larger and thinner. Would they flap in the wind?

'It rained all morning, but the sun is shining now.'

That sounded so beautiful I almost cried. I pushed my hair off my face.

'All you need is a bath and a cup of tea.'

My stomach retched and acid burnt my throat. I coughed.

He hesitated, held my arm, helped me up, eased me off the bed and led me to the bathroom.

He smelt of cleanliness: washing powder and aftershave.

'Oh! No bathtub! Have a shower! It'll do you good. Take

off your PJs first!' He gave me fresh underwear, a pair of jeans and a T-shirt, then closed the door.

I stood in front of the mirror, trying to figure out what I was supposed to do. I inspected the toothbrush as if I had never seen it or used it before, squirted some paste and put it in my mouth. The unfamiliar act had to be relearnt one stroke after another. Then I rubbed my body with soap, as if it was someone else's, and washed it down.

Deodorised and dressed, I stood on the pavement waiting. Andy spoke to Charles, the receptionist, put my suitcase and rucksack in the boot of his car, then helped me into the passenger seat and fastened the belt across me. The car smelt of chocolate caramel.

'Are you all right?'

I nodded my head and breathed in his scent.

'Off we go, then.'

We raced through the narrow streets of London. Everyone seemed to be driving against the traffic. I ducked whenever a bus swerved towards us.

'Welcome to England! We drive on the left. What's the big deal?'

After an hour of negotiating heavy traffic, it began to ease off and the sky got brighter and the scenery greener.

He sighed. 'Finally, we are getting out of London.' He gave me a chocolate bar. I broke off a piece and put it in my mouth. The gooey middle melted on my tongue and the smell of vanilla rose. I remembered the 'caramel caress' in the Black Magic box, which my mother had hidden in the suitcase in the loft for twenty-five years. They were so precious to her she couldn't eat them or let them go. What was left had been fat and dead white worms. How foolish! She neither preserved his memory nor enjoyed their taste! I ate, watching England go by: sheep, electricity pylons, back gardens, farmhouses, supermarkets with car parks full, derelict factories, lakes, tower blocks and overflowing rivers. A man ran after a child in a playground, picked him and flung him up in the air. He would remember that for the rest of his life. Would he be abandoned?

'Are you all right?'

'Yes.'

Who was this Andy? Was he an honourable man? Where was his house? What if he had lied to me and he was not living with his mother? He seemed relaxed and sang with the radio, 'I could use somebody. Oh-oh-oh – wha-ah-ah.' His black hair was thinning at the front, his eyes bright blue, his nose fine, lips generous and, if you ignored his silly ears, he would look attractive. He negotiated the traffic skilfully. His fingers, gripping the steering wheel, had fine hairs on them and they gleamed in the sun. He was wearing a black T-shirt with *Stop Whaling!* printed on it in red letters, jeans and trainers. He tapped his feet to the rhythm of the song. 'Someone like me!'

What would he do when we got there? Lock the door then undress me? Would he use force? I'd never seen a naked man before. Were they hairy, like animals? I overheard my grandmother once say, 'When it's up, they cannot think. They just run after their prey.' They couldn't be rational when aroused. I held the door handle with both hands. The best thing to do was to wait until we got there, refuse to go into his house, take my luggage and run.

'Almost there. This is Bedale's town centre.'

Small, beautifully decorated shops, a café with cakes in the windows, a butcher and a bank. I spotted a pub with a bed-and-breakfast sign. Was there a police station somewhere? Deflated, I realised that I couldn't ask the police for help, no matter what. I untied then retied the laces of my trainers, wiped my hands against my jeans and prepared to sprint out of the car as soon as it stopped. Andy turned into a cobbled road, parked in front of a wooden gate, switched off the engine, checked his pockets and got out.

Before he walked round, I leapt out. 'I want my suitcase.'

His mother, coiffed and aproned, opened the gate. 'Crumbs! Here you are!'

'Hello, Mother! Sorry we're late. London traffic.' He offered me my suitcase.

I shook his mother's hand.

'Najwa, my mother.'

'Please, call me Jane!'

'*Tsharrafna* . . . Pleased to meet you.' It was disrespectful to call mothers by their first names.

She smiled and directed me to the 'pigeon loft'.

'We converted the barn for our guests.'

It was an old stone cottage with wide windowsills, a kitchenette and an iron stove. 'The bedroom is upstairs.'

I went up and put my suitcase down gently on the shiny wooden floor. The old bed was spacious with pillows and cushions covered in embroidered white linen. The scent of lavender and soap filled the room. I bent down and sniffed the bedspread. I could hear parts of their conversation.

'She's foreign and frail,' Andy said.

'Poor lamb . . . Any family?'

'Not that I know of.'

'When . . . her health.'

'It might not be . . .'

I went down. The fire in the stove was lit, brightening up the room. 'Let me teach you how to keep it going. Close the damper, stir the fire with this bar and then put more logs on top. When you are done, open the damper.'

His mother stood outside the door, hands in pockets. 'Dinner will be served at seven. Please, come next door!'

'Aha! You can listen to BBC3 on the radio, if you like.' He switched it on and music as gentle as water rippled, rose up and filled the sitting room. I sat on the generous sofa and watched flames rise, fall, change colour: orange, red, gold, blue. Birds sang their farewell to the day outside on the oak tree. Warm, safe and surrounded by people I sort-of knew, I fell asleep for the first time in days, hugging my grandmother's shawl.

Andy woke me up gently. 'Dinner is served.' His hair was wet. He must have had a shower.

I washed my face in the sink, dried it, inspected my skin in the antique mirror and tied my hair back with a rubber band.

Andy watched me.

We walked to the cottage next door. The kitchen was warm and full of the aromas of beef, herbs and garlic, which was similar to the smells you would find in our kitchen back home. The shelves were full: mugs, plates, photographs of family members and memorabilia. I sat at the solid wooden table, which filled the middle space.

'Beef bourguignon. I hope you like mushrooms.' Andy's mother wiped her hands against her apron and pushed her glasses up.

I was about to call her 'Andy's mother', the way we did, then hesitated. 'Jane. It smells delicious.'

'Would you like some wine?'

'I cannot . . . don't drink.'

Andy gave me some orange juice. I drank half of it in one go.

They laughed. 'You must be thirsty.'

We sat down to eat. 'There is some wine in the food. I am sure it has evaporated by now.'

'No problem.' My secular mother would have been proud of me. My fundamentalist father would punish me for this.

The food was delicious, the beef and vegetables tender. Andy's mother sliced some home-made bread. 'Fresh. I baked it this morning.'

The sun streaked through the top half of the door, which was open. Was that my mother? Was she standing outside by the rose bush, waving at me? I choked.

Andy gave me some water.

'Now for the *pièce de résistance!*' Andy rubbed his hands together.

I understood *resistance.*

'My mother's apple pie.'

Jane poured some cream on my slice and gave me the plate. I bit into it. Nothing came remotely close to this, except my grandmother's home-made baklava with walnuts. 'So tasty!'

'I cook the apples with brown sugar.'

'My grandmother is a great cook.'

'You must miss them.' She collected the empty plates.

'I do. My grandmother went away to do the haj, my mother died of stomach cancer and I've never met my father.'

'It's a warm evening.'

'Yes. The good weather held up.'

'Yesterday the neighbour's ginger cat stood outside the door meowing. You know him – Buster.'

'Yes. You mustn't feed him, Mother. You're messing up his diet.'

Why were they talking about the weather and cats? Did I offend them by telling them about my family? Perhaps I shared too many details with them. Was that frowned upon in their culture?

'Tea?' Jane poured some milk into a cup.

We drank tea and spoke about Adeline, their late cat. They had buried her under the rose bush outside. 'She was lovely, furry, sweet and always licked my toes.'

'Do you remember when she hid under the sheets and we looked for her for hours?'

The conversation about the cat went on and on. Animals were so important in this country. Back home, cats lived with us but remained outdoors. They drank from the garden pond, ate leftovers and gave birth in basements. But they were never seen as members of the family.

After a week of good weather, great English pudding with rude names – spotted dick, jam roly-poly, jam tarts and banana custard, and hours of boring conversations about cats and dogs, my insomnia was cured and was replaced with constant sleepiness. I dropped off even while standing.

Wrapped in a blanket, sipping a warm cup of milk with honey, watching the glow of the fire, I would drift off to sleep. Then I would wake up to the smell of fresh coffee and the sound of sparrows singing their welcome to the morning.

I had a shower, changed and ran next door for a cup of herbal tea and home-made croissants. Jane thought it was better for me to avoid caffeine for the time being. Andy, comfortable by the fire, watched us eat.

I told Jane about my father and how he had left us when I was three years old. 'My mother fell apart so my grandmother took over. She raised me.'

'Lucky, that.'

'After the death of my mother, she advised me to sell the family's gold and go and look for my father. It would be really bad for my reputation to live alone after she dies. Shameful.'

'Shameful?'

'No one would get married to a woman who lived on her own.'

She laughed. 'That's one third of the population of England tarred.'

'Is it OK for women to live on their own?'

'Yes. Not a problem.'

'That's good. I might end up alone here.'

'Not an attractive woman like you, surely? You'll be swept off your feet.'

That night, Andy came to visit me in the 'pigeon loft', holding a large glass of wine. We sat at opposite ends of the sofa and spoke about the weather. I was curious about him. 'So what do you do?'

He rubbed his right ear. 'I'm a mechanical engineer. I help install hydraulic presses.'

'What are they?

'They're used in manufacturing many things. Bricks, for example.'

'Interesting?'

'Boring and mechanical sometimes. It puts food on the table.'

He ran his finger round the lip of the glass then licked it.

'Can I have a sip? I am curious.'

'Are you sure? Curiosity killed the cat.'

'Yes.' It tasted like vinegar with a tinge of sweetness.

He put the glass on the table between us.

'So you didn't work in Afghanistan?' I took another sip and coughed.

'No. I volunteered during the holiday.'

We were silent. I listened to the rhythmic sound of rain, the rattling of shutters and the barking of dogs.

'May I touch your hair?'

I tilted my head towards him.

He stroked it. 'Najwa, you're so beautiful.'

'I have a crooked nose.'

'That makes you more interesting.' He moved closer and caressed it. It felt like sprinkling sugar on my skin. I shuddered. The scent of his aftershave, a mixture of lavender and watermelon, filled my nostrils. When he hugged me, his heartbeat reverberated through the thin fabric of my shirt.

Full of fascination and dread, I wondered what he would look like, feel like, naked. The blue of his eyes was flecked with gold and his lips were tinted with wine. When he kissed me, my callow lips tried to hold on to his, grip him.

The colour of his eyes deepened. He embraced me, then led me to the bedroom upstairs. I could feel the unevenness of his chest hair under the T-shirt. Silence, except for the classical music downstairs. As he turned to face me, his eyes appeared sunken, his cheeks hollow and his jaw darkened by the unshaven stubble. I wanted to say, 'I'd better not.' I knew I should turn away, pack and leave, but I stayed put. My thighs ached with the effort to stop them from wrapping themselves around him. He slipped his hand through my shirt, cupped my breast and tweaked my nipple. Tremors of pleasure and pain rushed down to the centre of my pelvic cavity, there, where all nerves met. I paled. He buried his head in my chest and rubbed his bristly face against me.

It happened on Sunday, at two a.m., while the pigeons were asleep. Andy stripped quickly, joined me in bed, turned me over and kissed me. His fingers explored, probed. Suddenly I unravelled and, like a vase hitting the floor, I broke into pieces. Tufts of hair, puckered skin, lumps and protrusions, some drooping and others firm, pressed against my pubis. I panicked. When he slid into me, my treacherous body welcomed the invasion. I tilted my head to the west and let out a cry. It happened like this on a rainy English day. Nothing could stop it now: neither my mother's advice nor my grandmother's warnings about predatory men. Andy held me as I rocked in bed.

Relaxed yet flushed, he seemed younger. I held his head with both hands, the way that young woman had done in the café in London, and kissed his ears. We made love again. Andy was gentle. 'You must stop me if you're sore.'

'I'm fine.'

When we finished, he hugged me. 'You must miss your dad.'

How can you yearn for what you never had? 'I hardly knew him. I only remember his hands.'

'Any idea where he is?'

Going against the instructions of Gulnar, my contacts in Kunduz and Abu Alaa, I breathed out, then told Andy everything.

'So what was on the SIM and the SD cards you gave to this Abu Alaa of the Islamic Deliverance Front?'

'I don't know. Must be something dangerous. I must not tell anyone.'

Silence. No Aha or What's the big deal?

He stood up, got dressed and cleared his voice. 'You'd better ring that number.'

'I will tomorrow.'

His eyes shone in the morning light. How attractive he was! A strong urge to get up and touch him, lure him back into bed, took hold of me. I got up and walked towards him.

He stepped back.

208

'Andy?' I pleaded.

His shoulders slumped and he rubbed his ear. 'My mother is going to France soon. You need to find alternative accommodation.'

I shook my head.

'Goodnight.' He left without a second glance.

The next day, I didn't see his mother at breakfast. 'She had to go to town.' He put my suitcase in the car and we drove to the station in silence. I wanted to thank him for what he and his mother had done for me. They'd glued me back together. I wanted to say that I was sure my grandmother would be eternally grateful to them and that my family – what was left of it, that is – would never forget their kindness. I wanted to tell him that he looked so attractive in the glow of the fire. But Andy was in a sombre mood, so I remained silent.

He put my suitcase on the pavement and rubbed his jeans. 'I do hope that you'll find your father.'

'Thank you.'

'I've got to go.'

'Andy?'

His eyes were sunken, shoulders hunched and jaw set when he walked away.

I stood on the platform, waiting for the train and shifting my weight from one foot to the other. No kiss, hug or a proper goodbye. Why was he so cold with me? My grandmother had said that men were predators. 'You must not give yourself on a plate to them before they knock on your front door and ask for your hand in marriage.' Was that the way people did things in this country? Did men lose interest in women after they had slept with them? Or he might not have wanted to get involved with a foreigner. Perhaps he didn't approve of women travelling without an escort. But I went to Afghanistan to look for my father. Could it be the forged visa or the SIMs and SD cards? Whatever it was, it had turned me into an untouchable. It could be my father again. Who would want the daughter of a terrorist? I bit my lip until it tore and blood seeped out and spread, tart and sour, on my tongue.

Leeds, July 2007

My flight out was at eleven a.m. I was packed and ready to leave. Having performed my ablutions, dressed and perfumed myself with essential oils, I stood on the mat about to do my Morning Prayers. It was four a.m. when I heard a bang. Armed police officers in combat gear had kicked the door down and broken into the house. They were so similar to the American soldiers in Afghanistan, except for the colour of their uniform. I raised my arms in surrender. 'Allahu akbar.' They pushed me to the ground, then handcuffed me.

They searched the property and confiscated computers, documents, mobile phones, CDs and even coffee mugs, storing them in plastic bags and putting them in boxes. They also went through the house with a sticky rod and brushed everything, even the taps. I was a combatant in captivity, yet I was really impressed with their calm and thoroughness. If we had been somewhere else, my teeth would have been kicked in by now and my face trampled. The neighbours would have been here, shouting questions at the police. Some would have tried to free me.

When they'd finished, they led me out and, as the street watched from behind closed curtains, they put me in an armoured van, then locked the door. The journey was not too long. When I got out, I was blinded by camera flashes. I could not see where I was going. They led me into a building, down a long corridor, and put me in a small room, perhaps two square metres and shut the door.

Then the interrogation began. I gave them the names of all the dead jihadists I knew. They tried to break me – sleep deprivation, isolation, confinement in a tiny space – but, as a medic and a combatant, I'd been through so much it was impossible. I'd fasted for days, walked through prairies, looked for Hani among piles of corpses, turned a four-limbed baby into a bundle with no hands or feet, thrown human parts to dogs, dug out dead girls. There was nothing they could do that would even shock me. So I repeated the names of the deceased again and again.

The trial was conducted like a fine machine. All were calm and collected, including the wigged prosecutor. First, they appointed a lawyer to defend me. How shocking is that? If it were Afghanistan, then I would have been beheaded with a blunt sword. The lawyer said that my chances of getting justice in this country were slim because of the wide media coverage of the case. 'The jury has been compromised already.' Also, because my English was poor, I couldn't understand the laws of the land. I do speak excellent English – that is why I was chosen for this mission. They went on and on, exhibiting one piece of evidence after another: had traces of nitrate they found in the house, chemicals that proved that controlled explosions were carried out there, radicalising leaflets, lectures by extremist imams, etc. To my surprise, they haven't sentenced me to death, but to one life imprisonment, because I am fifty-two. Exhausted, I'm relieved that I don't have to go through the self-examination one has to do before death just yet.

The guards who got to know me were civil and kind. I was transferred to a prison in London somewhere. And there my hell began. They took my forged Pakistani passport and strip-searched me. A light was shone into my nostrils, ears, mouth, navel, and at my penis. They asked me to manipulate it before they examined it. I refused. A prison guard said, 'I'll do the honours,' and began to massage it. They inspected it for hidden drugs. When he stuck his finger inside my rectum, I knew exactly how Hani, may Allah bless his soul, had felt. It was worse for him because they penetrated him with a broken Pepsi bottle. The prison officer twisted his finger, probed, then fisted me. 'Did you say he masterminded the 7/7 attacks?' he asked the officer as he stuck his nails into the lining of my intestines. I bled for days after that.

When you're violated, you lose the self you are familiar with, the one you have conversed with for years, and a stranger knocks on your door and moves in with you. How do you learn to breathe the *different air? I tried to settle in, but there was always the hell of other people. White prisoners taunted me. 'Towel-head Muslim! Carpet-kisser! Sheep-shagger! Wife-beater!' They bumped into me 'accidently' and ridiculed the way I prayed. Once, a tattooed prisoner spat in my dinner. Because his saliva was najas – impure – I could not eat my lunch and went without food until the next morning.*

I was told that one young Muslim prisoner was bullied so much that he hanged himself. When I asked to be transferred, the officer coughed phlegm and spat it in a tissue.

One morning, while having my breakfast, someone grabbed me from behind and threw me down. I had been trained to defend myself, but I was fifty-two and out of practice. My facial tissues were flayed, nose and ribs broken and my ankle was twisted. Compared to the cases I'd operated on, this was minor. I was taken to hospital and treated for my injuries. A nurse with an open, honest face, cleaned my wounds, realigned my nose and placed a gauze pad inside my nostril. I have never seen blue eyes at such proximity.

My lip was stitched, so it was difficult to speak. 'I used to be a medic like you.'

'You what?'

'I trained as a nurse.'

'Never!'

'Why "never"?'

'You don't strike me as an angel of mercy.'

'I've saved thousands of lives.'

'You've inflicted so much suffering on so many innocent people.'

'No; you inflicted so much suffering on so many innocent people.'

'Me?'

'Not you; you. Your people.'

'Was that woman with the burnt face responsible for killing people God knows where?' She drew the curtains.

I think, because they were not dark, I had never noticed blue eyes before – never registered them. They had belonged either to a general, soldier or mercenary, but never to a nurse.

'No, but her elected government was.'

'She probably didn't even vote for Tony Blair.'

'Still guilty by association.'

'In this country, there is no such thing.'

She put her instruments in the kidney dish, put the clinical rubbish in the bin and left.

They put me in solitary confinement after that attack, then decided to transfer me to another prison. Handcuffed and shackled, I walked through the corridors. Inmates spat and shouted abuse at me.

'We told them about you. There'll be a welcoming party waiting for you, you filthy raghead.'

'They'll shag you like a woman, on arrival.'

'Hope they lynch you, you scumbag.'

'They disembowel paedos. They'll do the same to you.'

In an armoured car with four policemen, the journey up north began.

★

The train to Leeds arrived. I put my suitcase in the rack and sat across from a couple necking. Andy wouldn't even say goodbye. I put my mobile phone and the sandwich I had bought on the table. The thought of not seeing him or his mother again was unbearable – a slab of concrete, heavy over my chest, as my mother used to say when she couldn't go to sleep. I showed my ticket to the conductor. One departure after another: Amman, Peshawar, Kunduz, Kabul, London, Bedale. A bank of grey clouds spread at the end of the horizon, where some trees stood in a row. *Oak, pine, carob, cedar, lemon, jasmine,* and I breathed out. How neat England was! Andy cut me out of his life like a deft butcher, trimming off the fat. Any signs of distress were not allowed because they might attract attention. Dry-eyed and tight-lipped, I watched the clouds gather then disperse.

When I rang the number Abu Alaa had given me, a man answered, then the cross-examination began. 'What did you say your name was? Who gave you my number? Omar Rahman's whereabouts? Are you alone? How do I know you are his daughter?'

I pleaded with him to help me find my dad. I said *dad*, which was the way Andy had referred to his late father.

He seemed hesitant. 'I don't know you from Adam.'

I gripped both lockets. 'It's important. Please.'

He repeated the same questions again and again.

'He has a scar at the end of his left eyebrow.'

215

'I'll meet you in front of the Town Hall in Dewsbury at four p.m.'

A man in a striped suit was sitting next to me, reading a pink newspaper. Every now and then he lowered the paper and stole a glance at me. Was I being watched? I sat up and read the book, which Jane had given me, on Britain's endangered wildlife: *151 species of plants and vertebrates 'in serious danger of extinction' and another 328 species 'threatened'*. I looked up *vertebrate* in the dictionary: *Joint of the spine*. I read on: *Animals with an internal skeleton made of bone are called vertebrates. Vertebrates include fish, amphibians, reptiles, birds, mammals, primates, rodents and marsupials.* So animals with a backbone are under threat. What about humans? They have a spine. Am I an endangered species?

When we arrived in Leeds, I got off, put on my jacket and tightened my shoelaces, then tied them. The gentleman in the striped suit watched me. 'Where are you heading?'

Dewsbury must be north. 'South.'

'If you're stopping in Leeds on your way back then call me. I would like to take you out to dinner.'

He was elegant, blond, his skin creamed and perfumed. Why would someone like him want to take a woman like me out? Unless he was after something. Perhaps he wanted some information about Muslims. He smiled, showing even, white teeth, gave me his card and, to his surprise, I took it and put it in my pocket. 'Slut!' my mother said. When he disappeared

216

into the crowd, I read it. I must look up *barrister* in the dictionary.

The blonde behind the counter of the information desk eyed me. 'Take the Huddersfield Metro line. It's the fourth stop.' She was right to look at me like that. I was a foreigner, an invader of her country, and had no right to be here. If I were her, I would report me to the police. I bought a ticket and dragged my suitcase down the escalators and through the maze of passageways and platforms. Looking at the map, which resembled a spider's web, I suddenly felt really tired. My heart pounded, the muscles in my right cheek twitched, my palms were sweaty and my shoulders knotted. Who was this man I was going to meet? Would I be able to trust him?

A young man helped me put my suitcase in the Metro carriage. I sat next to a veiled Asian woman. Would I look suspicious sitting next to her? If I got up and sat at the front, I would attract more attention to myself. They might think I was trying to avoid her because of her different dress code. Were we all being watched? I took the paper bag out of my rucksack and ate the slice of apple pie Andy had given me yesterday. I chewed it, then swallowed. It went down the oesophagus, which my biology teacher thought was a miracle because it was a muscle continually contracting to push the food down, slowly.

When I arrived, I followed his instructions to the Town Hall. He said that if you drew a straight line from the exit of the rail station through the houses, you would find it. I walked by the main road, pulling my suitcase behind me, its rattling wheels disturbing the peace of the suburban neighbourhood. I looked through the arched windows of a honey-coloured villa. It was bright and full of chandeliers. What would I give to have been born on the other side of those walls in one of the lavish bedrooms. I would have had a mother, a father and perhaps brothers and sisters. Here, fathers didn't disappear to join some jihad that they had nothing to do with. I rubbed my fingers, took hold of the handle again and pulled.

I arrived at a town square dotted with trees and benches. Baskets full of flowers were hung on the street lamps, which were old and ornate. I sat to catch my breath. A man with short ginger hair, blue eyes and a beard, holding some blue prayer beads, appeared suddenly and sat next to me. I smoothed my jacket, mopped my brow, tucked my hair behind my ears.

He counted the beads. 'You must be Najwa.'

His voice was deep and smooth like that of a muezzin.

'How did you know?'

'You look like him, *masha Allah*.' He smiled, revealing chipped front teeth.

'My father . . .' My heart stopped. I cleared my throat, coughed and breathed out. 'You have met him.'

'Yes. Sheikh Omar Rahman.' He watched the traffic.

I held on to my rucksack. 'You're not just saying this.'

'No.'

'Really?'

'Yes.' He caressed the prayer beads.

'Where?' My voice was hoarse now I was close to the end of the trail.

'I was inside.'

'Inside?'

'Yes. Inside. A guest of Her Majesty.' He winked.

'I don't understand.'

'In prison.'

'That where you met him?' My English abandoned me.

'Yes. Inside.'

'Is he in prison?'

'Yep.'

'My dad is in prison.'

He nodded and counted his prayer beads quickly. The beads clicked against each other.

You were also a criminal; an abandoner, traitor, deserter of wife and child, saviour, fighter and convict. Great! My anger welled up. I came all this way, risked everything, probably criminalised myself in the process, only to find you behind bars. I sucked both lips and bit hard to stop myself from falling apart. The best thing to do was to put all of this behind me, take a train to London and fly back home. What else could I do? That nearness, that embrace I had craved all my life was not possible. Here we were. All the histories, politics and laws of the world had conspired against me, us. I clasped the handle of my suitcase, about to get up. The ginger-haired man held my arm. I tried to release it, but his grip was strong.

'Let me buy you lunch and tell you a little bit about Sheikh Omar.'

'I have to go.'

His face relaxed when he looked at the clouds. 'Please. Allow me to repay him for his kindness.'

'His kindness?'

'Yes.'

He picked up my suitcase and walked away. I rushed after him. We ended up in an empty café. It had wooden tables and chairs and weird winding plants in black pots. We sat in the corner.

'There is nothing halal here, so it's better to stick to vegetarian food.'

What would a strip of bacon add to my sins? I'd travelled miles and miles on my own, had wine and allowed a strange man to touch me. 'Fine.'

We went to the counter and he chose a mushroom and red onion pizza. I didn't recognise the food in the containers, so I ordered a potato salad and orange juice.

'We'll come back for desserts and coffee later.'

Put off by the smell of eggs, I toyed with the food.

'After the shock you've had, you need some sugar in your system.' He munched quickly.

I fished out the potato cubes, tried to wipe off the mayonnaise, then ate them.

Silence, except for the sound of our chewing.

'My name is Edward. My grandmother had a crush on the king. Everyone calls me "Red Ed". Please, call me Ed.'

'Ed.'

He ate another slice of pizza, looking at the traffic through the window. When he'd finished, he wiped his mouth. 'Your old man is kind.'

'My old man?'

'Your father.'

'How old is he?'

'He must be in his early fifties.'

One photograph I had of you was when you were probably twenty: sideburns and flared trousers. My grandmother said that it was two years before you got married to her daughter. Another photograph is of you in full Taliban gear, standing behind a poppy field. In my mind's eye, you were still young with curly hair and bushy brows. I couldn't imagine you old.

'The judge decided that I had tried to kill my girlfriend. They put me in prison. I was nineteen with no family to mention; you know – a foster kid.'

'Foster kid?'

'My mother was a heroin addict and they gave her methadone to help her stop. I was born an addict. Then, one foster home after another . . . That's the way it was.'

'Did you kill your girlfriend?'

'I loved her.'

'So?'

221

'No.'

I twisted my father's wedding ring around my thumb.

'Prison was strange: one iron gate after another; keys and locks. And the yards are tarmacked and bleak. Not a single flower. If you were lucky, you'd be allowed to go to the library, where you could have a glimpse of the clouds through the small window. That's it.'

'When did you meet my father?'

'Three years ago. It was my first week in prison. I craved methadone. Light-headed, nauseous, stomach cramping, I rocked in bed. Then I heard a beautiful voice reciting something. It was like a Gregorian chant.'

'Was it my father?'

'Yes. It went right through me, spreading peace and tranquillity. I slept.'

What would I give to have been lulled to sleep by you.

'Yes, strange.' He nodded. 'Just like that.'

I took a quick sip of the now-tepid tea.

Ed rubbed his beard. 'Later on, I discovered that he was reciting verses from the Qur'an.'

'Past midnight?'

'Yes, in the small hours, when the gates of heaven are open.'

This Englishman used prayer beads and believed in Muslim heaven! How strange!

'I met him finally on one of the courses. He was tall, with a salt-and-pepper beard and gentle smile. My heart trusted him instantly.'

'Salt and pepper?'

'Grey hair.'

The sun was setting outside. A woman took the ice-cream cone out of her baby's hand and wiped its face. It screamed. So you are old and I missed out on seeing you young. I wanted you to love me when you were strong and independent. Now you might pretend that you cared for me, because you're frail and old.

'He told me that he was reading the Solace: *al-Inshirah*. For the first time in my life, I was curious – good curious, that is.'

My mother made sure that I knew very little about religion. My grandmother sneaked in some *surats* and sayings in her everyday speech.

Ed cleared his throat and read in a watered-down Arabic with weak /a/ and /q/ sounds, 'Did We not widen your bosom? And relieve you of the burden – Which had broken your back? And We have exalted your remembrance for you. So indeed with hardship is ease. Indeed with hardship is ease. So when you finish the prayer, strive in supplication. And incline towards your Lord.'

It was the verse I had read in the mosque in Peshawar. The sun was too bright, so I shielded my eyes. 'Poetic.'

'Allah repeated "ease" deliberately.'

'He did?'

'Yes. I lived in my head most of the time – a lonely and messed-up place – and suddenly there was a higher force called Allah I could lean on. A companion, who'd travel with me this road less trodden.'

'Less trodden?'

'My life. Islam means surrendering yourself to God. I threw away all my baggage and put myself in His hands. Three weeks later, I converted.'

I was shocked. My mother's words were imprinted in me. Why would anyone convert to Islam? Why would anyone tie themselves in the knots of religion? Wear a veil! Pray five times a day! Fast during Ramadan! 'Why would you forsake your freedom?'

'I found the freedom and lack of structure in my life confusing. No one told me what to do or this is right and this is wrong. The self needs a framework. *Al-nafs ammaratun bil su*. You go haywire if there are no restrictions on you.'

'My mother said that religious people are backward. They believe in magic rather than scientific facts. We came into being by chance.'

'We cannot be here on this earth by accident. There is a creator for all of this.'

'It's easier, I guess, to believe in a god.'

'And harder. You have to worship Him and that's not always easy.' He sipped some tea and smiled. 'Also halal food was much nicer and we were given a long break for Friday Prayers.'

I held the mug with both hands, seeking warmth. 'Ed?'

'Yes.'

'Where is my father?'

'Your dad is in a high-security prison in Durham.'

224

'Durham?'

'A town up north.'

'Is it far?'

'No. Less than an hour by train.'

'Can I travel there today?'

'Yes. I'll drive you to Leeds.'

Part VI

Secret Whispers

I arrived in Durham at five o'clock in the afternoon. Praying costume – the gift from our neighbour in Amman – in suitcase, lockets around neck, father's wedding ring on thumb, grandmother's shawl in rucksack, stepmother's woven bracelet on wrist, dead half-sister's letter in pocket, I stepped out of the carriage. It was peaceful and all I could hear after the train had shunted its way out was the sound of wind and the rustling of leaves. The honey-coloured cathedral and castle shone in the sunset.

I followed the signs to the city centre to look for the B&B Ed had recommended. He told me that his sister had stayed there whenever she went to visit him. Both the breakfast and the landlady were really nice. He offered to come with me, but I turned him down. My grandmother said that you had to go through birth, illness and death on your own. Meeting your father for the first time must be added to the list.

The cathedral and castle were at the top of the steep bank of the river, dense with trees. I examined the map Ed had drawn for me, and dragged my suitcase over the slabs and cobbles of the bridge. The wheels made such a racket that the old men and women sitting on the steps around a statue of a man on a horse, eating chips, got annoyed. People watched me as I negotiated my way through them and up the opposite hill. Was it the colour of my hair, eyes or skin that made me look different? Perhaps it was the way I skulked, as if guilty until proven innocent. Did they all know that my father was a convicted criminal?

The house was square, with sash windows and a framed door with a porch. I rang the bell. A cat meowed, then came the sound of footsteps. An old lady with coiffed grey hair, large blue eyes and gold-rimmed glasses, wearing a frilled pink shirt, blue trousers and sensible shoes opened the door. 'Good afternoon!'

'Hello! I am Najwa.'

'Najwa!'

My name sounded foreign with the prolonged /a/ sound.

'I am Mrs Robson. Please call me Elizabeth. I've been expecting you. Ed's sister rang me. Come in! Come in!'

'Thank you.'

'You're so young!'

She shooed the cat and led me past the reception area to the sitting room.

It was decorated and furnished in shades of coral red. The colours and patterns of the rug seemed familiar. The two lamps on the side tables were definitely English. You wouldn't see them in our neighbourhood. We had plenty of light and didn't need extra during the day. I shook my arm, which ached from dragging my suitcase, and sat down.

Elizabeth pushed her finger into her buttoned-up collar. 'You must be tired.'

I nodded. The painting on the wall was of a white farmhouse in the middle of green fields. How tranquil!

'A cup of tea, then.'

She went out, came back carrying a tray and put it on the side table. 'I hope you like shortbread.'

'I don't know what it is.'

'Oh! It's made with caster sugar and lots of butter.'

I ran my fingers over the linen tray cover. So delicate! 'My grandmother embroidered napkins. She made me collars.'

'How wonderful! It's disappearing here; I mean, making things with your own hands.'

Her skin was puckered, brows grey, eyelids puffy and her fingers stiff, yet her warm smile stilled my heart. I unknotted my shoulder and savoured the first strong cup of tea I'd had since I arrived in England.

The Polish cleaner with grey eyes and peroxide hair carried my suitcase up the stairs to a 'room with a view.' I thanked Elizabeth and went up. It was simple, clean and fragrant. The bed was old and creaky, but the covers were mauve, my favourite colour. There was an old chair in the corner, a tall mirror on the wall and a glass vase full of white lilies on top of the covered radiator. The window above it was open. What a sight! Mowed green meadows slumped into the river, which wound its way through trees, boathouses and old buildings, all the way to the town. Ed had told me so much about the cathedral and castle, perched on the top of the hill on the right. He had visited them after his release from prison. How lush this Durham was! A black cow reclining on the opposite shore shone in the sun.

The garden beneath was full of plants climbing up the stone walls. One was in full bloom, with dark blue flowers, their petals velvety. I recognised a white jasmine and a honeysuckle at the far end. My grandmother had planted one by the steps leading to our garden and it grew quickly, carpeting the floor with its white flowers. My mother complained about having to sweep them every day. 'And the smell. I can't bear it!'

My grandmother sucked her last tooth. '*Tzzza!* Who would complain about the fragrance of jasmine?'

'The perfume is sublime.' I practised my vocabulary.

'It must've reminded her of him, the rascal.'

I closed my eyes and breathed in the scent of cut grass, trees and flowers, searching for a trace of your smell in the evening air.

For a few extra pounds, Elizabeth prepared dinner for me. We ate in the breakfast room. The tablecloth had a blue vase printed on it.

'I bought it from Mykonos five years ago. It's an amphora.'

'Amphora?'

'An ancient vase.' She poured wine into her glass. 'Do you drink?'

I didn't know how to answer that. I do – did – drink, but shouldn't and couldn't. Andy's burgundy lips nipped my nipple. I shook my head.

She put a chicken breast and some vegetables on my plate.

A familiar aroma. 'Thyme?'

'Yes; from the garden.'

The potatoes were crunchy on the outside and soft on the inside. 'Lovely.'

'I boil them, then roast them in goose fat.' She sipped some wine.

She unbuttoned her collar and pushed her glasses up. 'Najwa, Ed asked your father to apply for a visiting order. He told him that he was coming to Durham and that he needed to ask for his maximum allocations.'

'Allocations?'

'Yes. Prisoners have to agree to the visit.'

'Did he agree?'

'Yes; he thought it was Ed. Ed has a friend there. He's explained to him that you've come all the way from Amman looking for your father. He promised to help organise this surprise visit.'

'He might be too old for all of this.'

'Ed thinks that he'll cope.'

'Anything I should do?'

'Yes. E-mail your name, relationship to the prisoner and passport number to the prison.'

I panicked. Would they recognise the forged visa?

'They'll just check your name on the ID.'

I wiped my mouth.

'If you write down the details for me, I will send the e-mail this evening.'

'Fine.'

She wet her lips. 'It takes two days for your request to be approved.'

They seemed as long as all the months I had spent looking for you. I rubbed my chin, tucked my hair behind my ears, cleared my voice and repeated one of my grandmother's favourite proverbs, 'Patience is bitter but the outcome is sweet.'

Elizabeth stuck her forefinger inside her collar. 'What a glorious sunset!'

In the dusk, the shadows of trees outside seemed longer.

That night I couldn't sleep. The first time I realised I was different was when I was five. It was the Eid celebration and all the children of the neighbourhood were heading to the swings. The girl next door wore her new clothes, white frilled socks and shiny shoes, and waited outside. Her father, suited and perfumed, ran down the steps, stroked her hair and gave her some money. She kissed his hand, then held it. They walked together. I watched them until they disappeared out of the alleyway. They might go to a restaurant in the city centre to have stuffed lambs' necks, eat *kunafa* pastry with cheese or candyfloss. They would go to the park. She would fix a rubber band around her skirt and fly high on the swing for ten piasters.

I listened to Elizabeth cough a few times, seagulls squawking at four a.m., to traffic, distant and irregular, trying to guess by the swish of the tyre on tarmac the weight of the vehicle, its destination. The blackbirds rowed on the roof and the milkman's van rattled at six a.m. The sound of footsteps outside, then someone threw a *Good morning!* Was it English or Arabic? Finally the cathedral's bells donged. Morning dawned on Durham.

I told Elizabeth I wanted to go to the prison, even if they wouldn't allow me to go in. She rang Ed. He called his friend and he agreed to see me and explain the guidelines. I wore the two pendants, put all the empty perfume bottles and my half-sister's letter in my bag and went out. Before I jumped into the taxi, Elizabeth gave me something wrapped in a napkin. I thanked her.

Inspecting me in the mirror, the driver tuned the radio. He negotiated the traffic and repeated with the singer, 'Tears in heaven.' It would be great if I could cry. On the river's surface, just before a dip, broken boughs, feathers and twigs gathered. We drove up a steep hill, past a hospital, a big supermarket, then through a small town, with brick cottages and neat gardens.

'Here it is, petal.'

I paid him and got out.

You were so near, yet so far. A massive concrete wall which rose up, blocking the sky, barbed wire fences, dogs, guards and locked gates stood between us. What separated us was more than that: years and years of neglect.

The entrance was a door to the side. I went in and stood in the reception area, shifting my weight from one foot to the other. In the rush, I'd forgotten to ask for Ed's friend's name. 'Can I help you?'

'I applied for a permit.'

'When?'

'Yesterday.' Elizabeth had e-mailed them the previous night.

'It takes two days.'

Someone grabbed me by the arm and led me outside. 'Hi! I am Ed's friend.'

'How did you recognise me?'

'You look like your father.'

I composed myself.

He led me to the bench outside.

He was old, overweight and tired. He turned his head away. 'Eeh! Amazing resemblance!'

'What's he like?'

'Seems nice. He did some awful things, mind.'

'Did he kill?'

'You should ask him.'

He explained how thoroughly I would be searched and how I must leave my belongings in a locker, and said that I wasn't allowed to give my father anything.

'I just want to give him a letter.'

'I'll see what I can do about that.'

'Thank you.'

'No bother.'

The sun broke through. There was no green apart from a small lawn outside the prison. I sat down and listened. The chattering of guards, the sound of gates being opened, closed then locked, the clanking of keys, boxes being stacked and laughter. I pricked up my ears for the sound of your voice and sniffed the air searching for your smell. I stretched my legs on the wet grass and ate the piece of cake Elizabeth had given me. Reporting for duty, prison staff in white shirts and black trousers, gadgets tied to their belts, greeted me as they passed by. A dog barked somewhere. I tried to see what lay beyond the security fence, barbed wire and torchlights. Finally, we might be looking at the same sky, father.

Frankland Prison, Durham, January 2008

I have noticed the main difference between London and Durham: the temperature. It must be five degrees lower. And most people speak in an accent that I cannot understand. I try to tune in, but it takes me a long time to get the gist of what they are saying. Slowly, I have begun to socialise with other inmates.

One night, while I was reciting the Qur'an, I heard someone crying. I knocked on the wall gently so he could understand that I was not telling him off. He knocked back. I spent the night tossing and turning and tapping on the wall. The next day, at breakfast, Ed – a young, troubled man with blue eyes and ginger hair – came and sat next to me. I found the porridge tasteless, so I gave him some. He was still growing.

He smiled. 'Ta!'

'What does that mean?' I asked.

'Thank you.'

The great thing is that I understand Ed's accent.

First we began talking about the weather. How the trees by the river, which I haven't seen, will change colour with the seasons. He comes out with the most useless facts: Britain has 3,842 species of higher plants and 374 types of birds. There are so many breeding and wintering sites. Some birds end up here by mistake – like me, including ring-necked parakeets and mandarin ducks. We look for birds through the small window of the library, which we are allowed to visit sometimes. But there are no trees or plants to attract birds in this compound. And even if there were any birds here, they wouldn't fly as high as the library window. What is wonderful is that I can see rooftops and the sky. For a prisoner, a shred of sky is so precious.

One of the bombers in prison hooked up with a bad lot of gang members, those who slash necks and kill for either money or drugs. They have no principles. They've decided that, A: they are Muslim and B: they want to convert every prisoner to Islam. They began

238

harassing those who ate bacon or undressed in the showers. I watched them bully young inmates. 'You'll burn in hell because your wife is not a Muslim.' Brainwashing young men used to be my job, but suddenly I can see how ugly it is when it's done by others. To be bullied into religion is not our way. But why did I agree to do it?

I went to the gang leader and said to him that if he came near Ed, I would break his neck, vertebra after vertebra, with my bare hands, something I was trained to do when I was a toddler. They backed off, not because of my physical strength, but because of my reputation as a leader and a mastermind. They are afraid of the strings I can pull.

After that, Ed asked to borrow my copy of the Qur'an and every day he would come and tell me about a beautiful image or surat: 'When the Qur'an is read, listen to it with attention, and hold your peace: that ye may receive Mercy.' And, 'That Allah may reward them according to the best of their deed, and add even more for them out of His Grace.' And when he read, 'Never let your enmity for anyone lead you into the sin of deviating from justice. Always be just: that is closest to being God-fearing', he decided to convert. I need to get to know the self that advised Ed strongly not to do so. It goes against everything I stood for only seven years ago. My job was to isolate, convert, radicalise. Old age equals palpitations and doubt. And, before I knew it, Ed had recited the shahada and became a Muslim. I am too tired to present coherent counter-arguments against religion.

*

It began as a cough that kept me awake at night. Ed would tap on the wall his rhythmic support. 'Allahu akbar.' Then I began to get breathless and wheezy. The prison doctor prescribed a mixture, but it stirs the phlegm whenever I drink it. I am so tired I just want to go to sleep. I also get disorientated, thinking that my prison cell is back in Kunduz. I ask my second wife for fritters with extra syrup, then I tell off my first wife for keeping every perfume bottle I have given her or she has bought.

Najwa must be twenty-four years old by now. I dream about her walking through that cell door: a tall, majestic young woman with curly hair cascading down her shoulders. She would put her hand on my back. Just that. And my lungs would clear and heal. Then Amani would follow: a heartbreaker with Hazra eyes. She would put her hand on my forehead and all my inner turmoil would subside. In my old age I miss my wives, what they were and what they could have been, but above all I pine for my daughters. My wives simply come second. When I told Ed, his eyes filled up: shimmering blue lakes.

When the day I had waited for since I was three arrived, I didn't know what to do with myself. My father must be a strict Muslim and wouldn't approve of uncovered hair, make-up, a low-cut top or tight jeans. But my mother's ghost skulking in the room would be offended if I changed my secular appearance and hid my arms. My reflection in the mirror – gaunt, pale, with dry lips – stood between my parents' apparitions. I resented them both.

I wanted to look my best for this traitor. Applying some kohl, my hands shook and I had to wipe it off and start again a few times. Some of his converts might see me and my Western appearance might fill him with shame, so I compromised on the length of the top and wore the one that had belonged to my late half-sister, Amani. Gulnar had insisted that I should have it because the fuchsia flowers around the hems were embroidered by hand.

Elizabeth fretted over me. 'You must put something in your stomach before you go.'

I couldn't. 'No. Thank you.'

'Have you got the visit permit?'

'Yes.'

In her nightgown, hair dishevelled, she held her cat and stood in the hallway waiting for the taxi with me. When it arrived, she dropped the cat and opened the door. Just like that, she hugged me. Barely able to hold myself together, I stepped back, afraid that any act of kindness would push me over the edge, unravel me. I jumped into the taxi. She waved me off.

When we arrived, I joined the queue. Mothers with whining babies, fathers, reluctant teenage sons and grand-mothers carrying plastic bags stood waiting. When they checked my passport and permit, I thought that that would be the end of the journey. They might see the forged visa, put me in a police car, take me to the airport and deport me. With my luck the way it was, this could be it. I spread disease, death and destruction wherever I went. My father didn't love me enough to stay, my mother died of cancer and grief, my half-sister was blown into pieces and my stepmother lost her mind. The muscle in my left cheek twitched.

The prison guard gave me back my passport and a key.

Winded with relief, I almost fell.

'Please put your mobile phone, keys and sharp objects in the locker.'

Finger scanned, face photographed, I was led to the search area. The smell of musty shoes and sweat filled the airless space. I put my father's wedding ring, two locket necklaces, watch, money and key in a tray. My bag and shoes were X-rayed. I was instructed to go through a metal detector, then a woman guard padded me down. I blushed when I was spreadeagled and intimately frisked like that in public.

The guard sitting by the X-ray machine asked, 'What are these empty bottles?'

My English evaporated. 'Think my father gave to my mother.'

'Why are you taking them with you?'

'This is first time I see him.'

'The first time you've seen your father?'

'Yes. He left when I was three.'

He gave me my bag and waved me through. The woman guard who'd searched me led me to another reception area. 'You'll be accompanied by someone. You'll see your father soon.'

242

You were about to become flesh and blood. I paled.

She held my arm. 'Are you all right?'

I nodded.

A dog sniffed me. My grandmother believed that their saliva was impure and that you had to do your ablutions again if they licked you. My mother, who was in the kitchen hosing down the worktops, screamed, 'A fallacy!' The dog was large, with a long muzzle and a black nose. I stood still, suspended between my mother's science and my father's magic.

The visiting room had one window and was odourless, clean, with a few tables and chairs. The guards asked me to sit down and not to touch him or hand him anything. They stood to attention, then the door at the far corner was unlocked and opened. Ed had told me that my father was in a wing for enhanced prisoners and serious offenders. What did criminals look like? Men, clean-shaven, in T-shirts and jeans, fluorescent belts crossing their chests, rushed in. They were mostly white. Some had a swagger, others were timid, a few seemed relaxed, most seemed on edge, but they all looked normal.

I breathed out slowly, whispered the names of trees, and stretched my hands on the table to steady them. He was the last to enter. That old man couldn't be my father! I stood up and the guard, who was watching us closely, waved me down. He was tall, olive-skinned, bespectacled, bearded. A white crochet cap covered his bristly grey hair. Was that man my father? He paled, stood and inspected me. Hair frizzed up, face aglow with sweat, cheek twitching and hands trembling, I must have seemed unstable to him. When I bit my lip to stop it from quivering, he scratched his beard, turned his face towards the sunrays streaking through the window bars, then sat down, a total stranger. I lowered my gaze to my bag, full of empty perfume bottles, and my feet shod in white trainers. I twisted his wedding ring around my thumb.

'Najwa?' A silky voice. He took off his glasses, wiped the corners of his eyes, which were bright with unshed tears. The scar at the end of his left eyebrow was barely visible, his beard grey, cheeks blotchy, chin sagging, neck covered with moles, elbows scabby, and hands knitted with veins.

I had a sudden urge to leave all this behind me, travel back to my country, take care of my grandmother and keep her alive as long as possible. I was about to stand up. Then the area where my ribs met, and her blood trickled, felt warmer. I cleared my throat. 'Yes.'

He gestured something to the guard, who seemed flushed, and he nodded his approval. The betrayer, deserter, heartbreaker, absconder, traitor stood up, walked around the table, took hold of my arm, pulled me up and hugged me. His scent, unpleasant and familiar, reminded me of my mother. My head on his chest, I could feel his heartbeat against my twitching cheek. Then the warmth of his arms around my shoulders seeped through the fabric of my shirt. I remembered our neighbour's son's rejection and Andy's frosty farewell. Resentment welled up inside me and I stepped back. He sat down, took off his glasses again and wiped them.

I willed myself to be kind and to free my heart from all its fear, but couldn't. If only I could place my hand gently over his. But my mother rocked in her plastic chair in the garden, tranquillised, broken and bitter. I was angry with you and for you.

'I came here to give you this letter and leave.' Ed's friend had got me permission to give him one sheet of paper. 'It's from your real daughter, Amani. She's dead, by the way. My mother too. You killed her.'

He howled, flung himself at me, was restrained by the guards and pulled out. His screams echoed inside the prison and followed me all the way out and through the yard. Standing at the bus stop, I could still hear them.

Frankland Prison, Durham, June 2011

I have begun coughing up blood and every joint in my body aches. I know that the end is in sight. When you are about to embark on a journey to the afterlife, you tie your shoelaces and pack your bags. Alone I shall die.

Thoughts go round and round in my head. There is no decency or honour in what I have done. There is a schism between the man I hoped I would become and the man I finally became. Did I treat my late wife well? She was a good woman with one shortcoming: her desire to keep things as they were, to capture them. The death of her father at a young age must have stripped her of all feelings of safety and security; that's why, perhaps, she was controlling. Was that enough of an excuse to abandon her and my three-year-old daughter? Now she is dead my fickle heart craves her touch.

I missed out on Najwa's first day at school, her illnesses, happy events in her life. Did she go to school? She seemed educated, but heartless. What turned that baby, fluttering in my hands like a sparrow, into a cruel woman? I will never know because I was never there. I sent her many letters, gifts, photographs to make up for that lack. Can a word be a substitute for a touch? Perhaps she fell in love and it didn't work out. Maybe it is simple. With no father to protect her, she must have felt unsupported and became a psychopath, which is what one of the inmates has called me. I looked it up in the dictionary: someone with shallow emotions, who has no empathy, guilt or remorse. He uses others to his own end. But if Najwa is cruel, then I am to blame. Or am I? What makes us who we are? Events and people around us? Are we born flawed? Did I change? From a naive young man to a medic, then a wolf, who cannot howl at the moon anymore.

And even if Hani was tortured and violated by the secret police, I should have thought twice before leaving my country. I should have stayed and fought against that machinery that crushed everyone in its way. You don't liberate a country standing on the soil of another. How foolish of me. Young and trusting, we were duped, brainwashed and even exploited by the imams. The scheme

246

was larger than us and we, without the eyesight and perspective of an eagle, fitted right into it.

After Hani's death, Gulnar wrapped her legs round me for days in the hope that the warmth of her body would bring me back to life. She massaged my shoulders, washed my feet, cut my hair and trimmed my beard. I couldn't eat, sleep or speak. She rocked me in her lap, dripped juice between my lips, darted her tongue into my ear. Nothing. Curled up on the mattress, I wished for a drone, a sudden death. Then she wet my bottom with her saliva, blew on it, then bit me hard. I screamed, then I had sex with her for the first time in months. Her tears trickled into her ears. Gulnar restored me, stuck all the pieces together.

I wonder how she's coping with our daughter's death. I called you Amani – 'wishes' – because I had many dreams. If only we were able to create the cosmopolis we had desired. We searched for Xanadu, a place where nobody dared to go, far and wide. We found it inside our heads, then were claimed by it. If only the world was a better place, my half-Hazra daughter. You sat, your slit eyes gleaming, watching me make a doll for you. Then someone somewhere stepped on a mine, which was an almost daily occurrence, and I was summoned. I left the cloth doll naked and rushed out to stitch human skin.

Watching myself from a height, I can see that I was like an earthworm crawling from one dark ditch into another. I lived in the soil and dug myself in and out of trenches, from one reactive move to another, without much consideration or critical thinking. Earthworms have no eyes. And if you don't refrain, you shall not see.

*

247

Where is Merzad? My temperature has risen and a cold sweat has broken out all over my body. I shiver through another fever and crave a lethal injection to end it all. When Ed was here, he used to mop the sweat, a white hand over my dark forehead. I sob at the memory. I came to this country to punish the English for the death and destruction their army had visited on Afghanistan. A taste of their own bitter medicine. Yet . . . yet . . . Ed – white, ex-criminal – was like a son to me. I am fed, clothed, nursed by the English. Some are even kind to me, despite my dark deeds.

How did I turn from an angel of mercy to one of wrath? And is there an act big and meaningful enough to make up for what I have done? Is there atonement for a murderer like me? No. I pray for one bullet in the head to end it all.

I got better, but I am sure that I will pay for what I have done. My punishment is as big as my crimes: a prodigal daughter, bent on destroying me. Checks and balances.

I went back to the B&B, rushed upstairs, locked myself in the bedroom and refused to eat or drink. The father I had imagined was young and filled me with pride and this one was an old convict. The sheet of glass, which was my life, seemed stained and grimy. How could I clean it? Would the authorities track my forged visa and throw me in jail? Was my grandmother all right? Was she still alive? Our house had been left empty far too long. Had it been burgled? It might have squatters by now! Did my stepmother commit suicide? What was the data on the SIM and SD cards? Did they use the information to blow up a bus, train or aeroplane? Innocent civilians must have been killed. I stretched my fingers on the duvet. Did I have blood on my hands? Could I wash it off?

I had no energy. Talking was an effort. The Polish cleaner reasoned with me. 'Room will be *brudny*. Not good.' I massaged my face to ease the tic, wrapped the duvet around my ears and lay on my side, gazing at the wall. The room that had seemed perfect when I arrived was ugly. The walls had cracks running down them, brown stains dotted the white skirting boards and the pattern of the radiator cover had a star missing. The dark spot on the ceiling was neither a moth nor a spider. The mirror frame was chipped. The white lilies in the glass vase were fake and the water plastic.

The calls from Ed began.

'He speaks about you all the time.'

'*Her hair dark, spiky and her skin olive. Najwa is like a bulbul.*'

'He remembers clearly when you had a fever and he stayed up all night, applying cold compresses to your forehead. Your ribcage rose up and down in his grip.'

'When you were a baby, you loved mashed bananas mixed with orange juice.'

'You had your siesta on his chest.'

'You crawled out of your cot and slept next to him. You must've loved him when you were a baby.'

'How can you not forgive your dad? I wish I had a dad to forgive.'

Persistent banging. 'I shall keep knocking until you open this damned door.' Elizabeth sounded as resolute as my late mother. I dragged myself out of bed, stood in front of the mirror and stuck my furry tongue out. My grandmother had told me that hedgehogs pointed their spines at their enemies. 'Not to hide, but to fight. You have one spine, but pretend that you have many!' My hair was straggly, eyes sticky with discharge, pyjamas smelly, skin dry and itchy. I ran my fingers over my back, looking for evidence of some bone structure under the skin. I washed my face and opened the door.

'You silly girl!'

Elizabeth force-fed me an English breakfast: fried eggs, tomatoes, mushrooms, potatoes and baked beans. I tried to object but she wouldn't hear of it. After days of living on water, the fat floated in my stomach and lurched up. She seemed tired, eyes bloodshot, skin flushed, but her hair was coiffed, shirt ironed and buttoned up, and walking shoes shiny. She was ready for action. 'I can see how you defeated the Germans in the war.' My facial muscles ached when I smiled.

She threw her head back and laughed. 'Now, young lady! Get dressed!'

'Do I have to?'

'I need someone to do two afternoon shifts at the reception. Do you think you can do that?'

The money I had brought with me was running out fast. 'Yes.'

Some mornings I woke up shaking with anger and others I woke up soaking wet. Then shame gripped me: I had held my mother responsible for your departure, had hated her and hadn't even cried at her funeral; I had left my grandmother behind; I had allowed my half-sister's lover to kiss me and had given my stepmother a hard time. What if I was guilty of unspeakable crimes? I felt dirty. How could I let Andy, an infidel, touch me without a marriage contract? I must have a venereal disease. Some days I felt I was so contagious I could infect people at the other end of the phone, who were asking for rooms. I could barely write the dates in the record book.

As the days got longer and the nights shorter, I began to wake up early and go for a walk by the river just after sunrise. I took Herbert Edlin's book *Trees*, which I borrowed from Elizabeth's library, with me and tried to recognise some of them. How would anyone match words learnt at school, like *sindian*, with the living trunk, boughs and leaves of the oak in front of me? The coloured drawings helped me identify them. One morning as I stood by the river, looking at the water, which was seemingly still yet was rushing to the sea, I recognised the serrated leaves and red berries of an alder tree.

I followed the winding footpath, repeating, 'Alder, beech, birch, cedar, cherry, juniper, oak, poplar, rowan, willow.' On the other shore stood a tree with light green leaves that looked like a woman with her hair down, rather than tied up in a ponytail or raised in a chignon. When hit by the breeze, its colour got lighter, turned into silver, and its reflection in the river swayed. The boughs dropped right down and some plunged into the water. The book said that it was a weeping willow, but there was nothing sad about it. The white sap clung to the soil, and the leaves swayed happily.

I asked Elizabeth why the willow was called 'weeping'.

'Everything depends on your mood and perception. Some idiot believed it to be sinister and that it could uproot itself and stalk travellers.'

'Its roots must be tough, clinging to the edge like that.'

'They are. The Chinese take willow branches with them when they go to celebrate and honour their ancestors. They sweep their tombs, pray for them and offer them food, tea and chopsticks. Isn't that charming?'

'Can I make a long-distance call?'

'It'll come out of your wages.'

'That's fine.'

My grandmother should be back from the haj. I rang a few times and got a continuous beep. The line must have been cut off. Was she all right? Could she bear such an arduous journey? What if she had fallen ill or died in Mecca? Would they arrange a decent funeral? I'd have to travel all the way

252

there to sweep her tomb. How frail she'd looked as she climbed the steps of the bus, holding her best handbag, made of fake tooled-leather. Panic. I could not remember our religious neighbour's phone number. I wrote down a few, then crossed them out. When she'd asked, 'Don't you want to know my name?' I should have said, 'Yes.'

Finally I arrived at a combination that seemed familiar and dialled the number. Relief. Some Arabic through the static. '*Alo!*'

'It's me: Najwa.'

'Najwa? Oh! *Ya Allah!* Where are you?'

'In England.'

'Are you OK?'

'Is my grandmother back?'

'She's fine. Worried sick about you. I'll get her for you. Just wait! Please wait!'

Commotion, footsteps, children screaming at each other and then my grandmother Zainab's voice. 'Najwa, sweetheart?'

'Yes, Grandma.'

Snivels.

'How are you?' I said.

'I am fine now I've heard your voice.'

She must be talking to the neighbour. 'My granddaughter is in England!'

'How was the haj?'

'Oh! The lady took good care of me, may Allah lengthen her life. We got on really well.'

'I am glad, *tita*.' I'd never called her that before. Elizabeth hovered behind me, rearranging the box files.

'Did you find your father, sweetheart?'

'Yes, he's in prison in the UK.'

'In prison? A gentle man like him?'

'Yes. He also has a family in Afghanistan.'

'That explains it.'

'He had a daughter. She died.'

'I see.'

'I don't want to see him, Grandma.'

'It's time, my child, to see the contents of that box.'

'What box?'

'The box I left you. I wanted you to open it when you were about to meet him. You forgot to take it with you. Our neighbour found it in the garden and kept it for me.'

'Oh! Can you please post it?'

'Yes.'

'Grandma, I did some awful things.' Amani wept in the kitchen. Ashraf kissed me. A masked man gave me the sewing kit full of lethal data. Andy pushed his fingers into me.

'No one is squeaky clean.'

'Not even you?'

'Don't waste your money chatting to me! Hugs and kisses, granddaughter of mine. Give your address to our neighbour!'

'I love you, *tita*.'

'I love you too.'

'*Inshallah* we shall be united soon, if not in this life then the next.'

'God willing!'

My grandmother praised Allah in the background as I gave my address to the neighbour.

When I put the phone down, Elizabeth said, 'How is she?'

'She sounds fine. The trip to Mecca did her the world of good.'

'Good.' She put her anorak on. 'Can you man the castle? I need to go shopping.'

'Man the castle?'

'Take care of things for me.'

'Yes.'

She grabbed her handbag and left.

The Amman Tower had been different. The reception was 'manned' twenty-four hours a day and guests could come and go as they pleased. Here, everything was really organised. 'I will arrive at 11:45,' they would say. How precise! Back home they would specify the day, 'I'll arrive on Thursday.' That was good enough for the maid and the porter, who slept in the basement. Also, the owner asked the guests so many questions on arrival, for he managed a hotel to socialise. When I said, 'What do you do?' to a guest here, an old gentleman with a moustache, he corrected me: 'How do you do?'

I waited for him to go up the stairs, then waltzed with Anka, the Polish cleaner, repeating, 'How do you do!'

She smoothed down her uniform. 'How do you do, big boss?'

We laughed.

*

255

While I was highlighting confirmed bookings, the old gentleman, dishevelled and in a bathrobe, came running down. 'I cannot turn the tap off. The tub is almost full.' I switched the answerphone on and ran up. 'Call a plumber!' In Amman, we never called anyone if we could help it. I went to the bathroom and twisted the tap this way and that, but the water kept gushing out. 'Where are the mains?'

'Stopcock, you mean.' He twisted his moustache and watched.

I wouldn't repay Elizabeth's kindness by letting her house to be ruined. I asked Anka to cover the floor with towels and rushed down to the kitchen, opened the cupboard under the sink, swept cleaning products out of the way, stuck my neck in and looked for a large tap. Nothing. I ran my fingers over the plywood sheet at the back. Nothing. I tried again. Should I call her? I found a hole. When I stuck my hand in, it scraped against the uneven wood. Finally, my fingers hit cold metal. It was a large tap. When I cried, 'Yes!' Anka swatted the floor with her mop. I tried to twist it this way and that, but it was stiff. I stuck my wrist in and tried again and again. Finally, it moved and I turned it all the way to the right. The sound of running water stopped. When I pulled my hand out, my knuckles were bruised and my forearm was lacerated and bleeding.

I rushed back to the bathroom. Under the old gentleman's gaze I took off my shoes, hopped into the bath and unscrewed the top of the tap. Then, using pliers, I undid the nut underneath and teased the fibre. 'Get me some olive oil, please!' Anka came back running, her peroxide hair frizzed up. I dripped the oil on the nut, manipulated it, then screwed everything back. When Anka switched on the mains, I turned the tap on and off. All was fine.

The old gentleman seemed puzzled. 'You must've done this before.'

'Yes. Enjoy your bath! Screw gently, mind!'

'Screw gently? Preposterous!'

Later, Elizabeth inspected my hand and rubbed my forearm with antiseptic cream. 'You silly girl! You could've broken your wrist.'

Two weeks later, the parcel arrived. I took it upstairs and locked the door. It was the same shoebox I had left behind on the steps of the veranda. Still taped, it was wrapped in brown paper. The past, crammed in there for years, was about to pop out like a jack-in-the-box or a devil. I tore off the wrapping, removed the lid and emptied its contents on the rug. Shreds of old paper fell out. My grandmother's note, in her squiggly handwriting, said:

Whenever your mother threw his letters in the bin, I collected them, cleaned them and hid them in my wardrobe among my winter clothes. Searching bins and looking through rubbish became second nature. I also wanted to know what poison she was letting into her system. She wouldn't tell me what tranquillisers she was popping. This might not be complete, but it's what I was able to salvage.

Lots of love, your grandmother.

Letters, photos and cards fanned out around me as I sat on the rug on the floor. Some had been torn to pieces then taped together, others were creased and some were still unopened. Your handwriting was elegant and all the words tilted at the same angle in perfect harmony.

A drawing of yellow circles surrounded by daisies: *You must be five by now, sweetheart. I could not find a card. It's the war. They made this for you at the school.*

Another photo of you standing next to an ambulance, dressed in blue scrubs, your hair covered with a cap and your hands gloved: *I work as a nurse at the field hospital. The locals promoted me and decided to call me 'doktor'. I tried to explain, but the head of the village wouldn't hear of it.*

A knock on the door. 'A cup of tea and some biscuits.' Elizabeth stuck her head in. 'Have you finished that book I gave you?'

'Not yet. And thank you.'

I put the tray on the floor, munched on some shortbread and read on:

What is love? In Arabic it has many degrees: *shaghaf* is longing, *hub* love, *ishq* burning desire, *hayam* adoration,

258

gharam infatuation, *hawa* affection, *wajd* yearning (can be platonic), *shawq* longing, *wid* affection, *walah* obsession, *sababa* ardent. But there is no word for 'I love you, yet cannot live with you.' No word made of letters could describe my love for you.

A photo of a woman lifting a baby, swaddled in a white and green blanket with a wreath of flowers on its head, up in the air. She looked so young and proud. Could it be my stepmother? *Your baby sister weighs three kilos. A guzzler! Drinks, eats, pisses.*

A silver bracelet with *falak* engraved on it: *You must be fourteen, my daughter. I bought this for you. Adorn your beautiful wrist with it.*

Your mother does not answer my letters. How is she? Coward I am not, but I cannot muster the courage to ask for her forgiveness. I'll be devastated either way: if she grants it or denies it.

You must be fifteen today . . . Can you express your love in words? Is that sufficient? Can you express your beliefs in words? Is that sufficient? And how would you find a medium to describe commitment or its opposite? Is the word 'deserter' an adequate description of me?

You must be eighteen. A proverb: When your son grows up, treat him as you would a brother. I haven't heard from you. Are you getting my letters? If you are, why on earth are you not answering them? Do you hate me that much? I cannot come back, sweetheart. If I could, I would. Just to see your honey-coloured eyes and kiss your forehead.

I made this green star for you out of silk threads. It is the emblem of medieval Muslim kingdoms. With difficulty, I inserted it under the resin of the locket. I wanted something special for your eighteenth birthday. I do hope you like the shape of your name in Dari. One day, I will teach you some phrases. I am trying to say 'love' in as many languages as possible. A German journalist taught me 'Ich liebe dich'. I can also say, 'Je t'aime.'

I went for a walk by the river. The setting sun made Durham, its racecourse, cathedral and castle appear magical. Trees, windows, roads and the water gleamed in the purple dusk. The sound of leaves, catkins and nettles crushing underfoot comforted me. I crossed the river to explore the other side. The bridge, which was narrow and curved with iron railings, led to the old swimming baths. I walked past the public toilets, playground and the huge cricket field towards the boathouse. How could anyone feel shackled by the past in the middle of this vast green meadow?

I watched it from the other shore sometimes, dry, wet or glistening in the sun. There it was: a life-size cow or ox, lying down to rest by the river. Elizabeth told me that a group of monks were looking for a safe place to keep Saint Cuthbert's remains. Two milkmaids, looking for their lost cow, directed them to this place, which later became Durham. The cathedral was built around the saint's shrine and a high relief on the exterior of the north wall depicts two milkmaids and the dun cow. The bronze sculpture tries to capture all of that and more.

An inscription on the slab: Durham Cow. Legend would have you ruminating up by those massive piles, but what cow prefers a rocky mound to a riverbank? Here and now you seem real enough. I ran my bruised fingers over her golden horns. They were cold to the touch. Small and insignificant, I stood in the middle of all this greenness and brightness. Here and now, I – the skin, gristle, bone and blood of me – seemed real.

I went back, had a shower, changed, had breakfast and worked at the reception. Just before my coffee break, Ed's sister rang Elizabeth, who seemed distressed and kept trying to loosen her collar. She told her that my father didn't want to set his eyes on me again. 'But don't you worry! Ed is working on him.' Prisoners in Britain had the right to accept or reject a visitor and my father had refused 'point blank' to sign the permit. Ed told him that everyone deserved a second chance, even his own daughter, but he wouldn't hear of it. 'I am looking for a job. Do you think I should be hired? Then, like Prophet Muhammad, be kind!'

Elizabeth gave me a few more responsibilities and asked me to organise the accounts. It was a simple job of classifying then filing the receipts under different categories: expenses, food and drink, housekeeping, staff. Although I didn't understand notation or symbols, classical music grew on me. I wrote letters to my grandmother as I listened to Classic FM. I liked the advertisements for Mediterranean cruises that stopped in exotic places: Barcelona, Civitavecchia, Naples, Mykonos, Kusadasi, Santorini, Piraeus, Valletta.

Grandma, I imagine us on a beautiful ship – you, my mother and me – sailing through azure waters towards the sunset. The bedrooms are opulent, the food divine and the ballroom spacious. We eat, dance, sleep. Sipping mint tea and admiring Valletta, wherever it is. We shall meet, Grandma, Allah willing.

On my twenty-eighth birthday, Elizabeth gave me a thirty-pounds advance on my wages. 'Go and buy yourself something nice!'

It was warm when I walked down to the city centre. The river was calm and gulls dived then hovered. They knew how to soar solo. Perhaps they were born that way. Some blackbirds gathered on what must have been an ash tree.

'Faster!' the coach, in a funny hat, shouted at the rowers, training for a boat race. 'You can make it!'

I went to the ex-catalogue shop which Ed's sister had told me about, and bought a one-strap aquamarine top.

'Five pounds!'

I gave the assistant a ten-pound note out of my own earnings, beaming. If we ever went on that cruise, the top would be perfect.

She smiled and gave me back some change.

That was my first proper transaction in this country.

I walked back quickly, eager to show Elizabeth and Anka my top. As soon as I went in, Elizabeth, Ed, his sister and Anka shouted, 'Surprise!' Then they sang, 'Happy birthday to you, you live in a zoo, your dad is a monkey and you look like one too!' They laughed.

I sat down, breathless. 'My dad is a monkey. Do I look like one?'

Anka pulled her fringe down. 'It joke, you idiot!'

The table was laid out for lunch: salad, pasta, chicken, bread, biscuits, tarts.

'I made the Crown Royal cake,' Ed's sister said.

'It's so delicious.'

Ed wiped his ginger beard.

'He looks like the cat that ate the cream.' Elizabeth stuck her finger into her shirt's neckband.

'He's in love. She works at the Jobcentre.'

Elizabeth kissed me and gave me a wrapped parcel.

My gift was a frame, studded with pearls. Whose photo would I put in it? My mother's, grandmother's or father's? And would that make our relationship public, final? 'Thank you.'

That afternoon, I received a letter in the post. My father, Sheikh Omar Rahman, had agreed to see me. It felt like a date with a stranger. I had my hair trimmed and straightened, plucked my eyebrows, bleached my facial hair and put on Amani's shirt. Groomed, made-up, wrist adorned with the silver bracelet he had sent me, I went downstairs. Elizabeth smiled. 'You look lovely. Grown up.'

'Do you think he'll approve?'

'Yes. I would have you as my daughter any day.'

Durham was cold that afternoon, but bright. Shopkeepers stood outside scouring for customers. When I crossed the bridge, I could see some ducks gathered around tree trunks and twigs floating in the river. Leaves were losing their greenness and turning into rustic colours: brown, yellow, orange. Less chlorophyll meant aging then falling. There was so much beauty in twilight, a burst of the hues which are suppressed during youth.

While in the queue, waiting to be searched, Ed's friend came and said hello. 'It's good to see you again, Miss Rahman. Your father is better and is looking forward to your visit.'

'Better?'

'I'm sorry. Didn't you know? He was ill.'

With your death looming, I was suddenly free to love you. Omar Rahman – murderer, baby-abandoner, wife-jilter – was about to cease. Your treachery tucked away in the other life and your face hidden behind the horizon, any emotion was possible. The dam burst. Blood raced into my veins. It was hot in that confined place reeking of mould, cleaning substances and the breath of search dogs.

'I'm sorry. I shouldn't have told you.'

English words came out with difficulty. 'It better to know.'

My hands shook as I placed my belt, the empty perfume bottles, my necklace, bracelet, the wedding ring and watch in the plastic tray. My bag was full of photos and letters. Would the X-ray detect their history, the journey they were on, the broken promises, heartache? How could ink on paper make me ache like this? And how could memorabilia turn into stories and spin themselves around my wrists like shackles?

After being sniffed by a dog, I went through the numerous gates, then arrived at the visiting centre. My father was sitting in the far corner. He seemed thinner and older, his receding hair and beard almost white, his eyes vacuous, lips chapped and his arms covered with the red patches of psoriasis which I had inherited. Trying to stretch it into a smile, his mouth trembled.

I held his right arm, placed my lips on the protruding veins and kissed it the way good Arab daughters do. It smelt of soap, jasmine essential oil and you, Mother.

A perfectly shaped tear gathered at the corner of his eye – there, where the crow's feet meet. The guard signalled his approval. My father stood up, limped towards me and embraced me.

I filled my nostrils with his smell. My grandmother had told me about the locusts invading Palestine and eating everything during the drought and war of Safar Berlik. 'We dug the gold cladding out of our teeth and sold it for food.' It was over. My sharp edges, resolve, collapsed. I fingered my face: wet. My tears, bitter and salty, dripped down to my lips. I wept over the father who stood before me, a convicted criminal; my mother, who spent most of her life drugged and then died prematurely; our neighbour's son, who wouldn't get married to a girl brought up in a house without men; Andy's rejection; over my half-sister, who was desperate for my love and never received it, and over my stepmother, whose daughter's death unhinged her. I cried over my grandmother, who had lost her husband in the war, then her homeland, and who had to wait most of her life to do the haj. Cancer, death, suicide bombs, drones and blown-up buses. I howled.

His tall and spindly torso stooped and tightened its grip.

My mother always muttered under her breath, 'Who breaks a butterfly upon a wheel?' I could.

Then he said, 'Najwa.' It sounded right coming out of the mouth of the man who named me.

I wiped the tears with the back of my sleeve. 'Please, sit down! Your leg! What happened?'

He looked sheepish, even young. 'The day you visited me, I went crazy. Never happened before. Kicked everything: the bed, table, chair. Broke my shin. Then I got really ill.'

I swallowed. 'Amani was beautiful. This is her shirt, by the way. Gulnar gave it to me.'

He shook his head. 'You abandon one daughter, then lose another. Checks and balances. *They plot, but Allah is the best conspirator.*'

'A grand design, then.'

'It could be.'

I spread my memorabilia on the table. Under the watchful eye of the guard, I lined up the empty perfume bottles: Ramage eau de cologne, with azure top and a gold plate inside; L'air du Temps, with a dovescrew top; and Charlie.

He gawped. 'Where did you find them?'

'In a tin in the kitchen. She used to take a pink pill, spray herself with perfume and sit in the garden, thinking of you.'

His pressed his hands on his cheeks. 'So sorry.' His velvety voice had lost its smoothness.

'She couldn't get rid of them. She also kept all your things in the loft, including an untouched box of Black Magic chocolates.'

'I loved her. She was a good woman, but too wound up.'

'Is that enough of an excuse, Father?' My tongue faltered

over 'Father'. I showed him the wedding photo, my mother's hair gathered to one side. Then I got out the pearl hair comb with organza flowers.

'How innocent and unaware we were!'

'What happened? What made you leave?'

'Hani. What you don't know won't hurt you . . . or might.'

I pointed at the bracelet adorning my wrist. 'What does *falak* mean?'

'Fate, destiny. Allah has written our story.'

'What about choice? Do you think we can change what has been ordained?'

'Allah is the knower of all things; nothing exists outside of his will and decree. He inscribed all things in the preserved tablet fifty thousand years before he created the universe. A person is not forced to obey or disobey, but Allah can predicate our motives and deeds.'

'So, more or less, our life is mapped out.'

'Our characters are, therefore, our fate.'

'You leaving us, my travels and my half-sister's death are all part of a design?'

'It could be. Or as a result of the way I am.'

'A grand narrative?'

He pointed at my neck. 'You're wearing the locket. It passed through the iron curtain.'

'No; I found it in "your" suitcase after my mother's death.'

'I am sorry she's dead, Najwa.' He kissed my forehead.

I took the locket off and put it on the table. The foreign words inscribed on it and the embossed floral surround were uneven against my palm. 'What do they mean?'

'Najwa: a whisper or a secret conversation.'

'Why?

'At dawn and after Morning Prayers, I imagined you at four, eight, with ponytail and inquisitive eyes, asking me questions. I whispered my answers and blew them, hoping that the breeze would carry them to you. Also, life is a secret conversation.'

I clicked it open. On one side, a few emerald-green silk threads, arranged like an eight-pointed star, were held under the clear sheet of resin.

'I made that.' He tilted it towards the light. 'Such a symbol: Islam, Andalucía, the prophet's seal, the stamp of the caliphate. You can see this wherever the Muslims have conquered. We built octagon fountains and windows, and painted this shape on tiles. It encapsulates the balance between beauty and religion.'

He adjusted his leg, made a fist, then spread his fingers. 'Happy birthday!'

I tucked my hair behind my ear.

'You're so beautiful, sweetheart.'

The muscle in my right cheek tightened. I wavered between love and hate.

'I might not last long in this place. I miss Gulnar's fritters, the purple mist crowning the mountains, the open prairies. I miss my old job as a "doktor" and my assistant, Merzad. I want to be a healer again.' He gave me an old Qur'an; its green cover had embossed gold letters. 'It belonged to my father.'

It was my first holy book.

He kissed a dog-eared notebook, then pushed it towards me. 'My diary; a gift to you.'

Like a dirty tissue, I held it with two fingers, away from my body. What had he written? Why was it so precious? Could words change you? Should I thank him? Perhaps I should give it back to ward off the wrath of my mother's apparition.

The fabric cover was dirty and the spine stained. 'Hani's blood.' Additional notes, pages and photographs were clipped or slid between its pages. It was all held together with a rubber band. 'It's yours. My legacy, so to speak.'

As I fingered it, my mother tutted as if I were licking food off a dirty floor. Was it contagious?

'Recollected in rare moments of peace. Futile.'

'Futile?'

'Yes.'

'Here we are! Shooting stars.'

'Shooting stars?'

'They burn. Fleeting glimpse. We become human as we fall.'

He didn't make much sense.

★

270

That evening, over dinner, I told Elizabeth about my visit to the prison. She sliced the chicken and put it on my plate.

'He said that human beings are like shooting stars. They shine brightly then fall.'

She pushed her glasses up, wet her lips and stuck her finger into her collar to loosen it. 'Correct.'

'Do we all fall?'

'Yes.'

Her answers were brief. 'Are you all right?'

She looked at the setting sun through the window. 'Yes. Fine. Indigestion.'

'I'll clear the table and wash the dishes.'

She normally objected, but tonight she nodded her head.

It happened at six a.m. A thud. I rushed down to the sitting room and found Elizabeth on the floor, flushed, gasping for air, with her gown wrapped around her thighs. 'Cannot breathe!'

I sat down and rested her head on my thigh. 'Relax!'

Grey-faced and clammy, she convulsed on the rug. 'My heart's racing. Chest tight.'

I undid the buttons of her nightgown. She opened her eyes and looked at me. Her lashes were grey. 'If I had . . .' She coughed.

One of the guests rushed in in his pyjamas. 'Call 999!' He crossed his hands and pressed her chest. A grunt.

When the medics arrived, she was dead.

*

I stood by the window looking at the sacred cow for hours. A silhouette. A shadow with bright edges. A sculpture on the riverside. Anka knocked on my door. 'So sorry.'

No tears. The drought was back. 'Yes.'

'Good woman, really.'

'Yes.'

'Like a mother to all of us.'

She wiped her tears and closed the door.

Without thinking, I picked up my phone and pressed Andy's number.

A woman answered, laughing. Someone was tickling her. 'No!' she objected.

'Hello!'

'Don't!' Her English was elegant.

'Can I speak to Andy?'

'If you don't stop, you know what I'll do to you!'

Commotion, shrieks, panting. 'It's Najwa. Can I speak to Andy?'

'Naj . . . What? He's busy right now.' Laughter, then she hung up.

My hands were shaking when I put the phone down. Although it was midday, the Durham cow seemed pitch black in the distance. For a few seconds, I became a killer. If they had been in front of me, I would have knifed them. My grandmother's voice travelled over plains and seas. She repeated to my mother, 'In Allah, the best advocate, we trust. He'll settle all grievances and close all accounts.'

*

When I went to visit my father, I was full of cold.

With his beard shaved, hair longer and without his crochet cap, he seemed younger. 'Take some tahini and honey for that cough!'

'Is that good?'

'Yes. Soothing. Listen to your old man! He's a "doktor".' When he smiled, the crescent-shaped scar disappeared.

'How did you get that?' I pointed at my temple.

'I used to tease Hani so much. I once hid all the marbles he had won. He looked for them everywhere. Then he hurled himself at me and scratched my face. I was seven years old.'

When he laughed, I had a glimpse of the man my mother had fallen in love with, the one in flared trousers and sideburns. He seemed carefree. 'What changed you?'

'What do you mean?'

'What changed you from a Westernised man who loved jazz, to a . . . ?'

'Life, death, other people.'

'Dad, Elizabeth died.' I bit the inside of my lower lip.

'Yes, Ed told me. That kind landlady. May she rest in peace!'

'There is nothing left for me here, except you. But you're in prison.'

'I know.' He pulled at the sagging skin of his Adam's apple.

'Why?' I was asking him about his crimes.

'One day you'll forgive me for leaving you. Perhaps when I am dead.'

'Why?' I pointed at the guards.

'One should keep one's heart wired to one's head.'

'Will you ever be released?'

'Perhaps a few weeks before I die.'

'Then I should go back, make some money, save up for flights.'

'I think that's best.'

'But my grandmother won't hear of it.'

'Why?'

'She'll die soon, she said, and tongues will wag if I live there on my own.' I rubbed my right cheek.

He grasped my hand with his flaky fingers. 'I have one debt that I haven't cashed. It's long overdue.'

'You do?'

'I'll arrange for you to live with Hani's parents.'

'Will they agree to that? A stranger in their house?'

'Yes. You're like a granddaughter to them.'

'Did Hani have any children?'

'No.' He peeled a scab off the side of his knuckle.

'Long life to my grandmother! So when she dies, I can move in with them?'

'Yes. Taking care of you will rejuvenate them.'

'You loved him, Dad?'

He took off his glasses and wiped them. 'Too much, perhaps.'

'Too much?' I put my hand over his.

'One of Prophet Muhammad's sayings: *Ahbib habibak*

274

hawnan ma. Love those you adore with moderation, for they may be your foes one day. And hate those you despise with moderation, for they may become your beloved one day.'

Anka, Ed, his sister and I went to the crematorium to pay our respects. The coffin in the funeral car was barely visible behind the letters of her name, 'E-l-i-z-a-b-e-t-h', written with white roses. Two women, dressed in black, stepped out. The priest mopped his brow. A young woman stood by the door, tall, back bent, in a dress suit, her hair tucked under a black cap.

'Her niece.' Anka adjusted the flower in her lapel.

We approached them and introduced ourselves.

The hall had a glass wall overlooking a beautiful garden. The sunbeams lit it up and were broken up by the glass vase full of orange chrysanthemums on the piano into numerous little rainbows. I sat down, leant on the small rail cushion and moved the Bible away. No holy books for me. Dry-eyed, I listened to the priest's prayers.

Elizabeth's niece spoke about her resilience, generous heart, love of classics and her elegance, then played 'We'll Meet Again'. The soulful sound of the saxophone carried me to my father, the lover of jazz. He might be sitting in the library of the prison, his favourite place, reading about Edith Appleton, a fellow nurse. I'll be back one day to visit him.

The priest pressed a button and the coffin slid into an opening in the wall, then an electric curtain jolted and whizzed shut. No digging of graves, lowering of makeshift coffins, reciting of the Qur'an or wailing. Nothing, apart from the snivels and sighs of the mourners. I was able to cry this time. My cheek twitched. They all seemed composed. Embarrassed by the flood of tears, I rushed out.

The floor outside was carpeted with bouquets: lilies, roses, carnations, but no jasmine. Mine was a bunch of gypsophila, or 'baby's breath' as my grandmother would call it, which I'd picked from Elizabeth's garden and tied with Amani's red satin ribbon that Gulnar had knotted around my wrist before I left the compound.

'You're bound to us. Please come back.' Perhaps one day.

The morning sun magicked the wildwood: its trees sparkled and their leaves quivered in the breeze. The grass was freshly cut and its scent filled the air. Liberated by the spaciousness, I stretched my arms out and said to the chariot-shaped cloud, 'Peace be upon you, wherever you are!' After months of studying British trees, and much quizzing by Elizabeth over many dinners, I had begun to recognise them. The one I was standing under was a Himalayan birch. I could tell by the lenticels. The white bark was wrapped around the trunk like bandages. 'Wounded, yet standing,' she'd said.

I must go back to sweep my mother's grave.

Acknowledgements

First and foremost, my gratitude to my family in Jordan, Bahrain and the USA has no bounds. Your love, kindness and encouragement are what keep me standing whatever the circumstances. My fine Circassian mother's friendship and support are unparallel. Тхьауегъэпсэу *mama*! I am indebted to my brother Salah Faqir for standing by me. Many thanks to my brother Motasem, who facilitated a breakthrough in my research. I am also indebted to Wafa, Ekhlas and Eman, splendid professionals and the best of sisters. I must also thank my cousin Maha Said Al-Faqir for her kind support.

I am deeply grateful to Mike Daly, my first and discerning reader, Gwyneth Cole, Susan Frenk, Pat Barker, Isabel Cairns, Foad El-Dalaq, Ronak Husni and Gillian Boughton-Willmore in Durham, Samira Kawar, Yacoub Dawani, Louisa Service and Carol Seikaly in London, and Cora Josting in Berlin for their friendship. Your presence in my life is truly a blessing.

My friends in Jordan are too many to list, but I am grateful to each and every one of you.

A special thank you goes to the staff and principal of St Aidan's College, the University of Durham, where I hold a creative writing fellowship, for their professionalism and constant support.

I am also grateful to my students everywhere. Our endless discussions of the craft of writing fiction and literature keep my tools sharp.

This novel wouldn't have been possible without the Arts Council of England grant, which made researching the difficult and mostly undocumented terrain of this novel easier. The money, which is greatly appreciated, covered most of the cost of research material: numerous books and maps, and travel to conduct interviews here in the UK and Jordan.

Last, but not least, I would like also to thank my agent Toby Eady and his wife Xinran for their kindness, encouragement and continuous belief in my work.

HERON
BOOKS

Join us!

Visit us at our website, or join us on Twitter for:

• Exclusive interviews and films from
your favourite Heron authors

• Exclusive extra content

• Pre-publication sneak previews

• Free chapter samplers and
reading group materials

• Giveaways and competitions

www.heronbooks.co.uk
twitter.com/HeronBooks